Foul!

Paul Cockburn

Virgin

With thanks to Danny and Jack Shreeve and the boys of Remove B, plus Mr Ryecroft and Mr Owen, The Mall School, Twickenham, for invaluable market research.

First published in Great Britain in 1996 by
Virgin Books
an imprint of Virgin Publishing Ltd
332 Ladbroke Grove
London W10 5AH

Reprinted 1996

A catalogue record for this book is available from the British Library.

ISBN 0 7535 0070 1

Typeset by Galleon Typesetting, Ipswich
Printed and bound by
BPC Paperbacks Ltd, Aylesbury

Foul!

For Elaine:
she knows how much this all means

One

It was the scariest ride Jace had ever been on. He'd been to Disneyland and Universal Studios, but they were nothing compared to this. With each turn of the road, some new obstacle would loom up in front of the windshield of their 4x4. Sitting in the passenger seat, Jace would one moment be looking out over a long drop to the distant ocean, then next moment they would swing around another bend and a high wall of rock would be poised over the side of the road, waiting to collect them.

Jace knew this road well. His mother lived in LA; his father in San Francisco. Jace hated to fly, so whenever he moved from one home to the other, it would be down Highway 1, the long twisting road that connected the two cities along the Pacific coast.

The speed limit along here was a strict 50mph. His mum normally obeyed it strictly; his father might take it up to 60 if he thought there were no cops around. On some other roads, you might think of pushing on a bit more, but the coast highway was not a place for games.

He glimpsed at the speedo. They were doing 105.

He looked across to see if his mother was watching the dial, but her eyes were fixed in the rear-view mirror. That wasn't very comforting. Jace didn't dare look back himself. Instead, he kept his eyes forward, wondering how their lives would end – in a fireball as the car smashed into a mountain or in a long, tumbling drop into the ocean waves below?

The Cherokee hurtled round another turn, tyres screeching. Jace's eyes opened wide as he saw another car heading right at them.

That was a third option.

Overtaking was difficult along the highway. It was a narrow road – it had to be – snaking along the cliff tops, occasionally blasting its way through rocks it couldn't go round. Every mile or so there were places where slower vehicles were meant to pull over and let any traffic behind them pass through. Today, though, everything on the road was slower than their Cherokee jeep!

There was a white Toyota ahead, which had just pulled out to pass a dawdling Ford. The Toyota driver had taken advantage of one of the straighter bits of road for miles, clearly thinking there was nothing coming the other way. Their 4×4 was a big surprise.

There was nowhere to turn off, nowhere to hide. Three cars hurtled towards the same spot on the road, where there was only room for two. The Ford slewed on to the very edge of the road; the Toyota swerved across in front of it, its nose biting the road surface as the driver stood on his brakes.

Jace's mother flicked the 4×4 left and right, through the narrow aperture left by the others. They flashed by the two cars in an instant. This time Jace did look back to see the Toyota spin across the width of the road and the Ford run into its tail.

His mother gave a satisfied smile, her pony-tail snapping around like a whip as she turned to look back up the road.

'That should hold them up for a while,' she sighed. For the first time, she dropped their speed a little, down to a mere 95mph. The cliffs and rocks passed by a little more slowly.

⚽

Chris Stephens and Nicky Fiorentini were playing football-tennis on a hard court in Woodford Park. Using their heads and feet, they were passing the ball back and forth across the net, only occasionally seeking to beat the other player when a juicy volley sat up and begged to be smashed back. Mostly, they were happy to keep the ball under control, playing accurate passes back and forth between them. Two middle-aged men playing tennis on the next court but one glared at them jealously. They hadn't managed a rally that was half as long, and were never likely to.

The two boys kept up a steady rhythm, except for the few

occasions when one or the other mis-hit a pass, or when they both came close to the net to exchange rapid volleys and headers. Nicky was the quicker of the two; light on his feet, and quick to scamper back after anything that went past him. Whenever he had a moment, he pushed back his jet black hair, which he wore quite long. His teeth flashed in an almost permanent grin as he played the ball across the net, mixing delicate chips with flat drives that just skimmed over the cord. Every now and then he would deliberately stretch Chris by flicking a pass a bit wider or faster. Chris was too busy chasing the ball to do the same in return.

Across the net, Chris muttered to himself as he reached out to flick another pass back off the outside of his left boot. He knew that Nicky was starting to taunt him. It was just as well that Chris was taller and two-footed, or he wouldn't have reached half the passes Nicky sent him after. Though Chris was a little more solid than his team mate, he could move quickly when he needed to.

His blond hair was an unruly mess, but his eyes showed him to be capable of sharp concentration. Whereas Nicky had become a little bored of the drill they were using to sharpen up their passing skills, Chris hadn't lost his focus even a little. Of course, with Nicky mischievously making him work round the court, he couldn't afford to let his mind wander.

There were other things going on in his life that could easily have taken his mind off football. It was a bright spring morning and the season was drawing towards its close. Exams were looming up in the summer and Chris knew he was going to have to work hard after Easter to get some decent grades. He was having a good year as far as schoolwork went, but a few subjects were giving him grief – science and languages in particular.

Right now, though, that could all be forgotten. He could enjoy the warmth of this bright spring day and the fact that Wimbledon hadn't yet arrived to remind people that they had a tennis racquet in a cupboard somewhere . . . By June, these courts would be in use for about eleven hours a day, seven days a week. Right now, though, he and Nicky had plenty of space. Which was just as well, since Nicky seemed determined to make him run all over it.

Fortunately, he knew Nicky too well to let his mate's pranks put him off. During a game, Chris's judgement was almost faultless – he seemed to know instinctively where Nicky was about to place the ball. It was the secret of their success together. Right now, it meant that he could anticipate where Nicky might try to get him to run and be there early to meet the ball.

They kept up the exercise at full pace for another few minutes, by which time the two middle-aged men had paused to watch in admiration, gasping for breath from their own game. The boys had been working like this for almost an hour without even getting tired.

'Had enough?' asked Nicky, after he'd hit a lob past Chris into the back corner. Chris had chased back after it and hooked the ball over his head, but it had flown wide of the court.

'I suppose,' said Chris, glancing at his watch. Normally, he could keep this sort of thing up for hours – it was usually Nicky who got bored. Chris was a fanatic about football; he played at school, after school and at weekends. He played with his mates, he played with organised teams, and he would even make the most out of a twenty-minute kick-about in the garden with his father.

When he was much younger, Chris's father had taken him to a professional football match and he'd never gotten over it. Football was the centre of Chris's life and it was his ambition to play one day for Oldcester United. He and his father had season tickets at United's Star Park (Nicky had a third ticket – they always went together). A year ago, he had even played at the ground in the County Schools Cup Final, though the game had gone sour.

'What now?' asked Nicky, picking up his jacket from the bench at the side of the court.

Chris pulled on some track suit leggings and an old pullover while Nicky balanced the ball on his instep and flicked it up on to his head. Chris had never been much good at those kind of tricks, but Nicky was a master.

'I'd better get back and do some homework,' Chris said. It was nearly 11am. By 2pm, they would be at Star Park to see if Oldcester could get three points closer to promotion after just one season back in the Endsleigh League. In addition,

Chris had an important game for his club team, the Riverside Colts, on Sunday. He didn't have much 'free' time for the geography, maths and English waiting for him at home.

Nicky was grinning wider than before.

'What's the matter with you?' snapped Chris.

'I bet you spend an hour on the Net instead,' Nicky said. 'I would. Anything is better than having to write a report on some soppy book.'

Chris was no more keen on Jane Austen than Nicky, but he'd started writing the essay already and it wasn't too bad. He knew Nicky would leave it to the last minute.

'We've nearly got the Web page finished,' Chris said, letting his excitement show. 'Some mate of Sean Priest works in printing; he had a colour scanner, so we got these pictures of all the players –'

'All right, all right!' cried Nicky, holding up his hands to cut Chris off in mid-flow. 'I didn't want a three-hour discussion about it.'

Chris detected the sour note in Nicky's voice. His friend didn't know how to hide it when he was unhappy or angry.

'What's eating you?' asked Chris.

'Well . . . I thought you said I could help out . . .'

Chris lifted his eyes to the sky. He'd forgotten that Nicky had been keen to get involved. 'Sorry, Nicky. Look, why don't you come round tomorrow afternoon and I'll show you what we've got so far. Bring your Rothmans books with you – you can help me check out a few facts.'

Nicky brightened immediately. Ordinarily, you couldn't get him to look at a book short of nailing it to his forehead with the pages open, but Nicky was obsessive when it came to soccer statistics, and he owned a pile of reference books a metre high.

'OK! It'll be great to get out of the house for a while.'

'Oh?'

Nicky made an embarrassed 'Do we have to talk about this now?' kind of face. Chris remembered he was having problems with one of his cousins.

'OK,' Chris conceded. 'It's not a problem. You can come round my place for lunch.'

'It makes sense really,' said Nicky. 'After all, I'll only have to come round later to go to the football anyway . . .'

'Right,' Chris agreed, admiring the way Nicky had turned things round so that it almost looked as if he was doing Chris a favour. Fiorentini was grinning happily again now. If only every problem could be solved so easily.

Chris realised he'd spoken too soon when Nicky's expression changed to one of doubt. 'What are we having for lunch?' he asked. Chris sighed, and prepared to change his mind about that as well.

Almost halfway round the world, in California, it was the middle of the night and Jace was listening to the waves crashing on to the shore below where they were parked. His mother was fast asleep, having reclined the driver's seat back as far as it would go. Jace was sitting upright, looking out through the windshield at the dark trees beyond.

Shortly after the near-miss with the Toyota, they had pulled the Cherokee off the highway and followed a narrow track that had descended down through thick forests to a small camping area, from where an even narrower foot trail led down to the secluded beach.

There were a few other vehicles parked there, but none that Jace recognised. His mother had turned around in the small space and then backed the 4×4 between two tall trees so that it was hidden from the main parking area. Then she had turned off the ignition and they had started their long wait for his father to arrive.

Dusk had fallen. They had eaten everything in the cold-box his mother had had the sense to pack. They didn't leave the vehicle, except for a brief foray into the undergrowth when nature demanded. They heard tourists coming and going, but they saw no-one.

'That was a lucky encounter with those cars . . .' his mother had said, to fill the long silence. 'It gave us more time to lose ourselves. With luck, they'll drive halfway to LA before they realise that we're not on the road any more.'

Jace hoped so. He'd had just a brief glimpse of the men who had followed them out of San Francisco and he really didn't want another.

As night closed in around them, his mother had put on the radio for a while, with the sound as low as possible, listening to news broadcasts. Jace rummaged in his backpack for some comics he'd stuffed in there along with his camera, his GameBoy and his beloved 49ers baseball cap. Time dragged.

Finally, they heard an approaching engine. A car was moving down the trail very slowly, showing no lights. Jace felt his heart hammering in his chest and he saw his mother's hand hover near the catch of the glove compartment. Did she have a gun in there?

That made him even more nervous. He stared out of the 4×4, listening hard to the approaching car's wheels crunching on twigs and cones fallen along the trail, and the dull throbbing of its motor. It pulled into the small parking area beside the camp site.

It stopped. Jace caught sight of the brake lights through the trees and pointed them out to his mother.

They both waited with their breath frozen. After what seemed like an age, a torch flickered in their direction. It went out, then flashed twice. Jace felt his mother relax.

'It's your father . . .' she whispered, opening the door. She told him to wait, then leant back into the jeep and took the gun from the glove compartment. Evidently, she wasn't as sure as she sounded.

He watched her thread her way cautiously through the trees, disappearing from sight. There was a long silence.

Then two shots rang out.

Jace screamed in alarm and flung open the door on his side. His first instinct was to run to the parking area to find his mother. Then he heard a low, brutal voice snap, 'Find the kid!', and he dived into the bushes, sprinting hard away from the 4×4. He followed the edge of the parking area and found the track leading down to the beach. There was a little moonlight, just enough to see by. He plunged down the narrow trail at breakneck speed. He could hear the men behind him.

The track twisted and turned between sand hills and isolated trees, dropping all the time. It finally emerged alongside a small brook which trickled down towards a tidal pool. There was a long embankment beyond, which the trail followed. It was very open.

Jace ran as hard as he could, knowing that if he was spotted out on this spur of sand and rock it would be disastrous. He looked back only once as he reached the end and could drop down on to the flat beach, turning sharply to put the cliff face between himself and the trail. Crashing breakers obscured almost every sound, but Jace thought he heard someone yelling and another shot. The trail, though, remained empty. He hurdled some rocks and put it out of sight.

The beach stretched for almost a mile off to the right and there were gullies and small coves dotted all along the cliff face. Outcrops of rock that stretched to the water's edge provided even more cover.

The moon glistened off the rolling Pacific waves as they dashed themselves on to the flat sand. There were tracks all over; the afternoon tourists had spent their time in gainful exercise like all good Californians were supposed to do. There was no way anyone coming down to the beach would find Jace.

He dropped down in a small circle of rock that some kids had covered with sandy turrets to make it look as if it were a gigantic medieval castle. He had a clear view back to where the trail emerged along the embankment. Keeping low, he waited for trouble to appear.

It wasn't a long wait. Two men jogged slowly out along the path, puffing with the effort. One of them looked a little ruffled, as if he had tripped over on his way down the track. They both looked like they were auditioning for a part in a Tarantino movie, with dark suits, narrow ties and white shirts. No shades, though. They weren't that stupid. And they both had guns.

Jace froze, watching them carefully. They were barely 200 metres away, but he couldn't hear anything they said over the thunderous roar of the sea. Their gestures, though, gave away the gist of their conversation. The fatter one was angry and would have happily spent the rest of the night searching for the brat who had caused him to get wet sand all over his Armani suit. The skinny one with the spiked haircut whined about the size of the beach and pointed out how Jace could have gone anywhere.

Finally, the fat guy had to admit defeat. He kicked at the

sand and they both turned back to plod up the beach to the track.

Jace breathed a sigh of relief. At the same time, his heart was still gripped by a dreadful fear. What had happened to his mother? He had to find out.

Picking himself out of his hiding place, Jace followed the cliff back the way he had come, making sure he could duck back out of sight in an instant if need be. When he reached the corner, he peered round carefully. The two hoods were still trudging back up the trail. Jace watched and waited until they had passed back into the tree-line. He then forced himself to count to 50 before he set foot on the exposed embankment.

To his relief, it didn't turn out to be a trap. He ran the length of the embankment and slowly climbed back up the trail. As he reached the top, he saw that the parking area was lit up by the powerful headlights on three vehicles – the Cherokee (now pulled forward out of the trees), a four-door Cadillac and a police cruiser. The three vehicles were parked in a ring, each facing the centre. A tall man with grey hair tied back in a pony-tail was standing there, his gloved hands resting on the barrel of a hunting rifle. He wore a long, black woollen coat even though the evening was mild. The two goons who had chased Jace down to the beach were walking into the circle with their heads hung low.

'Did you find him?' asked the man. They didn't answer.

Jace's pulse was racing. He knew that voice! He'd heard it once before on his father's answering machine. He didn't know what the accent was, but it wasn't American. Nor did it sound like the way English people talked on the TV. Australian, maybe. Or European.

Jace knew one thing for sure. It was a voice that was at the centre of all his troubles.

He couldn't see any sign of his mother. Had she got away too?

'Idiots!' exclaimed the man. He picked up the rifle and tossed it to one of them. 'Take the jeep somewhere and torch it. Don't leave any evidence behind – do you understand?'

The two suited hoods nodded briskly and jogged towards the 4x4. They opened the doors, climbed in and started the engine.

The man waved them away impatiently. They revved the off-road vehicle up as high as it would go, then drove it away up the track, fishtailing from side to side on the loose surface.

The man remained at the focal point of the remaining pairs of headlights, watching them go. Then there was another voice.

'I could call the kid in as missing; get some search parties out here.'

The tall, grey man shook his head. 'Best if you keep a lower profile. I'll find ways to neutralise the boy. Meanwhile, we have to make sure that all the other loose ends have been tied up. Understand?'

'I know what I have to do,' the other man replied. Jace squinted, trying to filter out the bright lights of the Cadillac so that he could see the man standing by the police cruiser more clearly. He couldn't – the man had his back to him. Other than the fact that he was a big man wearing a police uniform, Jace couldn't make out anything about him.

The slender man with the pony-tail took a long look around the clearing.

'There's not much harm the boy can do to us. He's stuck out here for now and by tomorrow we'll have things back under control. If not, we'll catch up with him again as soon as he surfaces. After all, there aren't that many places he can hide.'

With that, he ducked his head and slid into the driver's seat of the Cadillac. The big car started up and then the headlight beams bounced and swayed as he turned it over the rough ground, heading for the track.

The cruiser followed it, but there had been that one moment, when the glare of the Cadillac's lights had swept to the side, when Jace could see the officer a little more clearly. His night vision had been ruined by the brightness, but he made out two details that stuck in his mind. One was the large signet ring the man wore on the little finger of his right hand; the other was a livid scar on the upper edge of his jawline.

The two cars disappeared up the slope, their engines finally disappearing under the continuous beat of the distant Pacific waves. Jace explored the forest as carefully as he could, but there was no sign of his mother. He found a spent shell casing near where the 4x4 had been parked, but that was all. Slipping it into his pocket, Jace searched himself to see what resources he had. He found $1.15 in change, another $5 bill in his wallet, some chewing gum, his keys, his camera, his baseball cap, his wallet organiser and a pen.

It wasn't much, but it was all he had. Somehow, he was going to have to find a way to turn the tables on the grey-haired man and his cronies.

First, though, he had to get out of there and find a place to hole up while he planned what to do. It wasn't going to be easy.

Two

'Easy! Easy!' chanted Rory, laughing.

Chris almost did a double take. Rory Blackstone, who played alongside Chris up front for the Riverside Colts, had just sounded more like Nicky than Nicky.

They trotted slowly back to the centre circle. Chris slapped Rory on the back.

'Nice header,' he commented.

'Ah, it was a great cross,' said Rory, grinning, sounding a bit more like his usual, modest self. Chris accepted the compliment and ran the moment through in his mind. He'd felt good about the cross the moment he'd struck it. It had teased the opposition goalkeeper into indecision and Rory had gone up at the back post to head in a simple goal.

Chris heard Jazz exclaim 'Nine-nil!' just behind him, as if he couldn't believe they were playing so well. The Colts had all been so tense and over-excited before the game that they had started badly. Russell Jones had made three good saves before the Colts launched their first attack. Finally, Chris had settled them down when he scored two goals in a minute before half-time. Since the interval they had been invincible, with a hat-trick for Rory, one for Jazz, and others for Polly, RJ and Mac.

There was nothing about the game itself that had made them so edgy at the beginning – North Bullton were bottom of the division with an appalling defensive record, while the Colts were top – but it had a deeper significance for some of them. At the end of the season there was a chance that some of them would be going on to join the youth scheme at Oldcester United. It meant the team would be broken up – once a player signed youth forms for a League team like

United, the only other team they could play for was their school.

This fact had dawned on the Colts as the season unwound. They had been looking like potential Champions from the beginning of the year and the games just after Christmas seemed to confirm that they were pretty near unbeatable. Chris had been playing the best football of his life.

They had a game over the Easter holiday which could win them the title. The prospect excited all of them but it wasn't the reason why they were all so high.

'I've not scored a hat-trick since junior school,' whispered Rory. He was beaming all over his face. 'I think I'm really coming into form!'

'It couldn't happen at a better time, Rory,' said Chris.

'We'll really show them American boys a thing or two, won't we, Chris?' his fellow striker observed.

That, of course, was the cause of the excitement. The Colts were taking part in an exchange programme with some American students that Easter – the American lads were due to fly in that afternoon.

The exchange was the brain-child of Sean Priest, the youth development manager at Oldcester United. Chris could see him sitting on the steps of the portacabin that provided the dressing rooms for both teams, watching the game with obvious delight. Sean had a special interest in the Colts, a team he had helped to organise along with its manager, Iain Walsh. It was a badly kept secret in the Oldcester District League that the Colts were a kind of reserve pool for United's youth squad, a place where players who were on the fringes of making the grade could play and train together.

The exchange had been thought up originally as something the United youth squad would take part in – a high school in Newark, New Jersey had written to Priest asking if they'd like to take part in a scheme where twelve American kids came to the UK at Easter, after which twelve Brits would go out to the USA in the summer. Unfortunately, United's youth players were taking part in a summer tournament, so Priest had hit on the idea of the Colts taking part in the exchange.

Competition for the twelve places had been keen. The Colts only ran a small squad, but – inevitably – someone had to be disappointed. For the rest, though, there was the prospect of two weeks' training at Star Park with the United team, a special tournament and a host of other activities. Not to mention the trip to the States for the 'away leg'.

It was the opportunity of a lifetime. Chris had almost managed to blow it when he had quit the team in the autumn in a ruckus over a new player. All that was forgotten now.

In fact, the only thing more likely to be forgotten at that moment was the game they had already won. Almost straight from the kick-off, North Bullton went upfield and scored a consolation goal.

'Want to bet Iain makes more of a fuss about that goal than the nine we scored?' sighed Rory, as he and Chris got ready to restart the game. Chris didn't think it was worth risking a single penny on.

In fact, though, the Colts' coach was in too good a mood himself to give them too much of a hard time over the goal. After the game, he went through the motions of asking if Zak could remember how many minutes a game lasted and if Jones had been to an optician lately. No-one was properly terrified, so he handed over to Sean Priest, muttering about the fact that they had a League game to play while the Americans were over and that they'd probably manage to lose it while their heads were in the clouds.

'What would it be like if we ever *lost* nine-one?' asked Jazz in a quiet whisper to the others.

'Pray you never have to find out,' replied Zak, the team captain, who had been with the Colts several years. Several of the team could remember what it was like when the Colts had drawn 2–2 in an away Cup game at the beginning of the season before, and some of them had been prepared to walk eight miles rather than share a mini-bus with Walsh on the way home.

'OK, pay attention,' said Priest. The players gradually hushed their chatter and turned to face him. 'Now, I've told you this twice already, but you lot are so dozy today, I'd better go through it again.'

'Is there something special happening, then?' asked Chris. Everyone laughed (even Walsh) and Priest threw an empty plastic drink bottle at Chris as a punishment.

'Did I mention to you that we might only be able to afford to send eleven players over to the States in August?' he joked.

'Mac will be gutted,' said Chris, and the gathering broke out into even louder laughter as Mac protested that it would be better if Polly missed out because none of the Americans would be able to understand his strange country accent. Polly said it should be Zak, Zak named Jazz, and the whole rolling argument was on its way round a second time before Priest could get them to shut up.

'OK, seriously,' he said. 'Their plane arrives at eight. I'm going down on the coach with Iain, Zak, Chris and Jazz. You three – be here at 5.30pm. The rest of you, be waiting here at 11pm. I want to see twelve smiling faces ready to receive their house guests. Tollie – you've only got another ten hours to tidy that pit you call a bedroom; Rory – make sure your mum buys plenty of groceries, because your partner eats like a horse. Everyone clear on all that? I want you all to be on your best behaviour, even though all you have to do is take them back home, feed them a snack and then get some sleep. Tomorrow, we meet here at 11am to give them a tour of the city, OK? Tuesday is free, then Wednesday is the first practice day.'

Chris could have recited most of the rest of the schedule by heart and he was sure the rest of them could have too. Even guys who weren't part of the exchange were looking forward to the fortnight.

'Sean, what happens if we don't get on with the guy you've paired us up to?' asked Tollie.

'No changes. Whoever the unlucky Yank is who has to stay with you and your sister, he's just going to have to survive it.'

There were a few other minor questions, which Priest answered quickly. It was clear he was just as excited as they were. Finally, things calmed down enough and he could escape.

'I'll see you all later. Good game today.'

With that, he exchanged a quick word with Iain Walsh, then ran off to his car. The Colts trooped off to get changed.

'It'd be really funny if one of us did get someone they

couldn't stand,' observed Jazz as they crowded into the small cabin.

'Get real, Jazz. They're not going to send us anyone really weird, are they?' replied Chris.

Which just went to prove that just because you're a great footballer, it doesn't mean you're any good at fortune-telling.

⚽

The 747 arrived on time and the visitors were through passport control, baggage reclaiming and customs in just under an hour. They emerged in a block, wearing matching blue and white track suits, black trainers, and baseball caps which bore the legend 'MOUNT GRAHAM HIGH' and a badge with a picture of an eagle.

There was one other thing that was immediately noticeable.

'Look at the size of them!' gasped Mac.

Mac was not a big lad and most people appeared gigantic alongside him, but Chris was smaller than all but a couple of the American boys. Two of them almost ducked going through the door.

There were two adults with them. One was a younger man, maybe 25, who was built more like Chris and his mates than an American – Chris even thought he looked familiar – and a fat, busy little man with an expression of permanent worry welded to his face. He caught sight of Sean and Iain, and quickly made his way over to them with his hand extended.

'Mr Priest, Mr Walsh. Pleased to meet up with you at last. I'm Benford Carter, and these –' He gestured to the close-knit unit of boys behind him '– are the Mount Graham High School Soccer Eleven!'

It was the kind of announcement that needed a fanfare to go with it. Mr Carter was clearly very proud of his boys. They, on the other hand, looked embarrassed by the fuss and stood in their little huddle, looking around at the airport as if they expected it to be more alien.

Actually, Chris noticed, they weren't all standing in a group. One of the boys was hanging back slightly, off to one side, clutching a small camera in his hand. He looked even more out of place than the others. He wasn't that tall, but he was very solid and looked more like a rugby flanker than a football player. He had a baseball cap drawn tightly on to his head, the peak obscuring his face. It didn't match the other guys' caps, though, but was in the red and gold of the San Francisco 49ers.

'Fancy meeting him down a dark alley,' muttered Zak.

'I bet he's your one, Jazz,' Chris whispered, stifling a chuckle.

'I hope not,' said Jazz. 'He'll eat my dad's shop by Monday.'

Sean and Iain had gone over to the American lads with Mr Carter, who introduced them. The American then brought forward the Newark team's captain – a tall, blond lad with a wide face and dark eyes.

'This is our team captain, Mason Williams the third!'

'The third what?' whispered Mac to the others.

'He's a sequel,' quipped Chris, also keeping his voice down. 'Didn't you see *Mason Williams Two*?'

Sean beckoned for Zak to go over. 'Mason, this is our team captain, Mark Pasternak, better known as Zak.'

The two boys mumbled something to each other and shook hands, managing to keep the contact as brief as possible.

Watching the small group of Americans, it was easier to believe they were waiting in line for tetanus boosters or dental appointments than the chance to meet their hosts. Chris felt every bit as awkward.

'We'll save the rest of the introductions until we get back to Oldcester, shall we?' suggested Priest, clearly keen to get out of the arrivals area as quickly as possible. 'Otherwise we'll be repeating ourselves all night. For now, let me just say that I'm Sean Priest, the youth team manager at Oldcester United. Welcome to the UK!'

A few of the Americans managed to get as far as 'it's good to be here' in a ragged chorus. That bit had clearly been rehearsed and Mr Carter looked slightly peeved that it hadn't sounded more genuine.

'Jet lag,' he said nervously, offering it as an excuse.

'Don't worry – I expect it's just a little bit strange for them,' Priest said. He raised his voice so the others could hear. 'Look, let's get out of this airport, shall we? I expect you could all do with something better than airline food to eat.'

'They fed them on the plane?' asked Jazz, softly.

'No wonder they needed a Jumbo jet . . .' Mac observed.

The Americans filtered through in a line behind Mr Carter, shuffling along like prisoners in an exercise yard.

'This looks like it's going to work . . .' muttered Chris.

'How did we get in touch with this lot in the first place?' asked Jazz.

The answer proved to be simple. Sean Priest had stepped back to allow the boys to pass and then walked over to the blond man, who was at the back of the group.

'Hi, Stefan,' he said, grinning. The other man was smiling broadly as well. They shook hands warmly.

'Sean – how are you doing?'

'OK, mate, OK. You?'

'I'm doing good.'

The accent gave it away. Chris realised who the man was now.

'That's Stefan Brodenberg!' he gasped, loud enough for it to carry to where Sean and the other man were standing. Sean looked round to see who had recognised his companion.

'I take it your young friend is a fan?' the blond man asked.

'I'm afraid so,' replied Priest. He called Chris over. 'Stefan, this is Chris Stephens, a pain in the neck who just might – might – be a decent forward one day.'

'Is there such a thing?' enquired the other man as he shook Chris's hand. 'I've always believed forwards were just cry-babies. Why don't you learn to play real football, in defence?'

It wasn't a serious question, which was just as well since Chris was finding it hard to think of anything to say. He'd heard stories about the legendary Stefan Brodenberg, who had played in the same Oldcester United team as Sean Priest. He'd been a Danish international, but his career had been winding to a close when he'd joined United for two years, instantly becoming a crowd favourite for his bone-jarring tackles. The fans at Star Park had nicknamed him 'Conan', after the movie with Arnold Schwarzenegger – Stefan's accent was almost identical.

'It's good to be recognised still,' the defender admitted. 'If English forwards are still silenced by the mention of my name, I must have made a big impact, yes?'

'Quite a few players around at the time can remember the

impacts you made very well,' commented Priest. 'They were pleased when we got promoted, because it meant you could dish it out to somebody else.'

Stefan turned to Chris. 'Did you ever see me play?'

Chris shook his head. His first game was the season after Stefan retired from the game. 'I've got a video, though. There's a game on it when we played Liverpool in the FA Cup. You marked Souness.'

'It was more like an American football game than real football,' Priest remembered. 'It's the only game I know where people remember the tackles more than the goals.'

'You're just sore because I got our equaliser,' said Stefan.

The rest of the party were making their way towards the exit, shepherded by Iain Walsh.

'So, what's it like teaching in the States?'

'Good. Better than here, I think. More money.'

'Tell me about it.'

'Newark is not such a nice place to live, but the school is in a good area, you know? Outside the city. And the boys love their football. They won the State final, you know?'

'You said . . .' replied Priest. He turned to explain to Chris. 'They won a competition to find the best team in New Jersey. The prize money and some sponsorship is what's paying for this trip.'

'So, when I knew we had the money, I thought where better to go for an exchange visit than England?'

'What he means is that they didn't quite have enough money for Italy . . .' Priest joked.

'Bah!' scoffed the Dane. 'Who can be bothered with all that Italian food? I want some proper food. Steak and kidney. Fish and chips.'

There was a McDonalds franchise at the airport, near the main doors. The American kids were looking through the windows.

'I mean it, Sean,' said Stefan, making a face. 'I want some real food.'

⚽

Stefan was a really easy guy to get along with, much like Sean in that he could talk to someone of Chris's age without sounding patronising. His job as sports co-ordinator at the American school was completely different to being a PE teacher in the UK. If 'Flea' – the sports coach at Spirebrook Comprehensive, where Chris, Mac and Jazz were students – heard about the facilities and support Stefan had, he'd die of jealousy.

'You and Chris know someone in common,' said Sean, as the coach cruised up the motorway towards Oldcester.

'Really?'

Chris realised who Priest was talking about. 'He means Peter Schmeichel.' Chris had got to know Manchester United's keeper when he went up to Old Trafford for a trial. They still kept in touch. After Oldcester's early ejection from the FA Cup in January, Peter had sent Chris tickets for Manchester's fourth-round tie against the team who had put Oldcester out, with a message saying that Manchester would show him how it should be done.

'You know Peter?' asked Stefan. 'Is he still the big joker?'

Chris nodded, grinning. Schmeichel had sent him a signed Manchester shirt after they had beaten Oldcester 5–0. The keeper had written '5–0 – ho, ho!' in marker on the front.

'We played together in Denmark a few times,' said Stefan. 'He was a crazy man then. I grew a beard once. He took my shaving foam and filled the boot of my car with it.'

They shared a few other stories, then Sean went off to talk with Benford Carter near the front of the bus, while Chris sat with Mac and Jazz, plus a couple of the American lads, listening to Stefan's football stories.

The journey passed quickly. Outside, the night was pitch black. They were on an unlit section of the motorway, heading north. A few isolated lights gave away the distant windows of farmhouses, but otherwise they were rushing through a featureless landscape in varied shades of blue and grey. The reading light above Stefan's head focused their attention on him like he was on TV in a darkened room.

'Just like American football, or rugby or any other kind of football,' said Stefan, 'soccer is about controlling the ball. If the other side doesn't get the ball, they can't score. Possession is the key. So, you need a good mixture of players who can get you the ball and others who can keep it for you.

'That's the problem in England. Your game is too fast now – everyone rushes everything. Even tackling. Easy tackles get missed, or you win the tackle but lose the ball again straight away.'

His audience listened carefully. Chris was very impressed. Stefan had a reputation as being one of the game's hard men, a no-nonsense tackler and a tenacious man-marker. Instead of him being some kind of thug, though, he was intelligent and articulate.

'There are England internationals now who throw themselves into reckless tackles and whine about getting booked. And if they get the ball, all they are good for is hoofing it upfield. The other team, they pick the ball up and come forward again five seconds later. That's not defending!

'I admire players like Stuart Pearce. You Americans, you should try to see Nottingham Forest play while you are here. Pearce is their captain, and full back, yes? Watch him carefully – when he has to make a challenge, it is hard, fast. Bang! The ball goes into touch, the attack is dead. But other times, you see him deny the attacker space. He slows the game down, waits to make a proper interception. That's because he knows that if he can win the ball cleanly and take possession, he has the skill to make a run up the flank, or a long pass. That is good defending.'

Chris looked up to see Sean Priest walking back up the bus along the narrow aisle, holding the luggage rack for balance as the bus swayed. He caught Chris looking up at him and flicked his head for Chris to follow him.

Chris got up and slid past Jazz to follow Sean to the front of the bus.

'That's how I like to see forwards!' mocked Stefan as he saw Chris go. 'In retreat!'

Benford Carter was sitting in the seat behind the driver with one of the American lads – Chris recognised him as the solid-looking guy who had stood apart from the others. Mr Carter still wore his worried expression – if anything, he looked even more concerned now than he had before. It was catching, too. Priest's face was looking pretty serious.

Chris sat with Sean on the other side of the bus.

'This is Chris Stephens. Chris, I want you to meet Benford

Carter, the principal at Mount Graham High School, and his nephew, Jace Carter.'

'My sister's boy,' added Benford very quickly, extending his hand to shake Chris's. His smile had a forced quality about it.

'I'm pleased to meet you,' said Chris, trying to make it sound welcoming. Jace was watching him warily. Chris recalled that his partner on the exchange was called Carter, too – Stockton Carter. 'I didn't realise Stockton's cousin was coming as well,' he added. In fact, the more he thought about it as he waited for the reply, he couldn't recall the name Jace Carter from the list Priest had read out a month or so ago. Bearing in mind he'd been told specially that he was pairing off with the principal's son, it seemed odd to Chris that nothing had been said about his nephew.

'Actually, he's not . . .' replied Benford. Chris flicked his eyes quickly at Jace, who was sitting sullenly in his seat, staring at the back of the driver's head. He was starting to get an odd feeling about all this . . .

'I'm sorry?' he asked.

'He hasn't come "as well",' explained Benford. 'He's come instead.' His eyes looked very sad for a moment and the lines across his forehead deepened. 'Oh dear. I'm not explaining this very well.'

Sean Priest, sitting in the aisle seat, turned to face Chris.

'Stockton couldn't come,' he said flatly. 'He's ill. Jace has come in his place.'

There was something unusual about Priest's expression that Chris couldn't quite decipher. He took another moment to glance again at the pale, almost sickly colour of Benford Carter's face and the stubborn set of Jace Carter's jaw, and decided that he didn't really accept that simple version of the story at all.

'I'm sorry to hear that,' he said. 'It's nothing serious, I hope?'

Benford managed a thin smile. 'No, nothing too bad. But infectious, yes. Infectious.'

Chris nodded as if he understood that this would rule Stockton out. 'Too bad – I expect he's very disappointed.'

'Oh yes,' said Benford. 'Very disappointed.' Chris noted how much more emphasis he gave those words. Mr Carter was clearly very well aware of just how Stockton felt.

He turned his attention to the frozen figure sitting in the window seat beyond his uncle.

'Still, it's good his cousin could make the trip instead. Keeps it in the family, right?' Jace Carter didn't answer. 'You must be pleased . . .'

Jace glanced across at Chris. 'Yeah, I'm *real* happy about it,' he replied brusquely.

Chris made the most of that moment of eye contact. 'Well, anyway, we're partners for the next couple of weeks. It's good to meet you.' He stretched his hand out past Benford Carter. 'I'm Chris,' he said, several seconds later when the American hadn't moved.

Benford nudged his reluctant nephew. Jace glowered up at him, then made a big point of putting his hand against the glass, cushioning his head against the vibration as the coach picked up speed to overtake someone.

'Yeah, right,' said Jace.

⚽

'So, what's he like?' asked Nicky. There was a fiendish delight in Nicky's voice that suggested he already knew the answer.

'Have you been talking to Mac?'

'No!' said Nicky. Chris could almost *hear* his grin down the phone.

Chris decided he couldn't be bothered getting Nicky to admit the truth. 'He's the biggest pain in the behind I've ever met,' Chris told him, which was saying something, bearing in mind he knew Nicky. 'He spends most of his time in the house up in his room, except when he's moaning about the food or moaning about the fact that he's already seen every episode of *Star Trek* or *Babylon 5* or *Home Improvements* . . .' He sighed.

'How did the tour round town go?' asked Nicky, sounding a little terse. Chris recalled that he had accused Nicky of much the same thing when the Fiorentinis had first got their satellite dish and Nicky had been able to crow about how soon they were going to be able to watch the fourth season of *Babylon 5*.

Chris took a deep breath and gave Nicky a brief summary of the first full day of Jace's visit, when they had joined the others for a coach ride around the city's landmarks and a foray out through the forests and hills to the north of the city.

'He sat on the bus the whole time. Didn't get out to look around the castle, didn't want to see the canal museum . . .'

'He sounds pretty sane to me so far,' said Nicky, who wasn't that enamoured of Oldcester's cultural offerings either.

'He carried his camera with him all day and didn't even take a single picture. The only time he really said anything was when he saw some horses and wanted to go riding. Sean told him there wasn't really time then and my dad said he'd find out about doing something later in the week.'

'Horse riding? Sounds exciting.'

'Well, that's about the only thing I know that he *does* like. Come on, Nicky. You *have* to help.'

Nicky remained reluctant, which showed how bad things were, since he had been only too keen to get out of the Fiorentini household at every opportunity since his older cousin Natalie had moved in at Christmas (she had landed a job as a make-up artist with the local ITV company, and was living at Nicky's place while she looked for more permanent accommodation).

'Look, this might sound a bit obvious, Chris, but have you tried talking to him about football?'

'Of course I have!' cried Chris indignantly, before he remembered that Jace might be able to overhear him from upstairs. 'It's no good. Half the time he looks at me as if I'm speaking a different language! I asked him which team he supported and he said the 49ers!'

'They're probably the best, Chris . . .'

Chris wondered if Nicky was doing this on purpose. 'They're not a football team, Nicky, not a proper one anyway. They're NFL! I don't think Jace knows anything about any football teams.'

'Well, what about the other Yanks. Can't he hang out with them?'

'He doesn't want to, and I don't think any of them are that bothered either. I know the kid staying with Jazz is meeting up with a couple of the others over the park this afternoon, but Jace doesn't seem to be friendly with any of them.'

'That's odd,' said Nicky. At last!

'So, will you get over here and lend me a hand?'

He waited for Nicky to make up his mind. Various bribes and blackmail schemes were beginning to suggest themselves.

'What's he doing now?'

'He's in my room, using the computer. I think he's getting some e-mail ready to send back to the States.'

'Ah! He's a cyber nerd, is he?'

'Maybe, I don't know. Anyway, are you coming over or what?'

After a little bit more hesitation, Nicky agreed to be there in half an hour. Chris put the phone down and went into the kitchen to wait for him.

His father was there reading the newspaper. He didn't have to be at work particularly early that morning, so he was hanging round to make sure Chris and Jace had plans for the day. Chris sat down beside him and finished the slice of toast he had abandoned.

'Sorted?' his father asked.

'Uh-huh,' Chris replied, trying not to commit himself.

'Good. If you go over to Nicky's house for lunch, Mrs Fiorentini can feed Jace. He might not like it any more than he likes what I cook, but at least he won't be hungry afterwards.'

One thing Jace Carter wasn't shy about was eating. In just one day in the Stephens' home, he had eaten half a week's groceries. Chris had never seen so much stuff crammed into just one sandwich before.

Once his father was on his way to work, Chris climbed the stairs to see what his guest was doing. Jace was at the computer in Chris's room, staring intently at the screen much as he had been when Chris left him.

'Would it be OK if I logged on now?' Jace asked, without looking up.

'I guess, for a while. I normally wait for the evening when the calls are cheaper.'

'Don't you have a local call connection?' Jace asked.

'Yes, but it still costs money.'

Jace screwed up his face as if he had just been told that people in Britain didn't have flush lavatories or mains drainage.

'You pay for local calls?' he sneered. 'What a crock!' He

thought for a moment. 'Look, I just want to send a few bits of e-mail, OK?'

Chris offered to show Jace what to do.

'It's OK. I've used Apple Macs and CompuServe before. I'll manage. Have you got a floppy disk I could use?'

Chris dug one out from a drawer and handed it over. Jace was already dialling the connection. Chris could hear the ugly squeal from the modem, followed by a busy signal.

'What's that?' asked Jace.

He wasn't happy when Chris explained.

'Just leave it ten minutes, then try again,' Chris said.

Jace muttered something and went back to working on his messages. Chris left him to it.

He had just finished clearing away the breakfast dishes when Nicky rang the doorbell. Chris had never been so pleased to see him in his life.

'Where's the boy wonder?'

'Upstairs,' said Chris, his voice quiet.

Nicky grinned. 'Can't even get in your own bedroom, eh? Never mind, I've brought the rest of that info you wanted. We'll kick him off the machine and finish preparing the United home page. Maybe he'll offer to help, if he's such an expert.'

'I doubt it,' said Chris. 'Besides, he doesn't seem to know anything about football at all.'

'I don't buy that,' Nicky replied. 'He plays, doesn't he? He must enjoy the game to be good enough to come on the exchange.'

'Well, he hasn't shown any interest at all in playing or anything. When I told him we had tickets for United's game on Wednesday night, he just yawned!'

They went upstairs. The door was closed again (Chris had left it open when he had left), but Chris wasn't about to be shut out of his own room. Nicky, laughing, asked if he was going to knock as they walked along the landing, which ensured that Chris just barged in.

Jace looked up with considerable irritation as they entered the room. Chris could see that he had logged on to CompuServe and was sending his e-mail. Jace made a point of putting himself between them and the screen so that they couldn't see anything.

'Hey,' said Chris. 'This is Nicky, a mate of mine from school. I told you about him, right?'

'Sure,' said Jace uncomfortably. He looked Nicky over quickly but didn't bother to introduce himself.

Nicky, however, had no qualms in a situation like this and strode across the floor to get right into the American's face.

'How's it going?' he asked, beaming, sticking his hand out. Jace looked at it suspiciously, then reached out to shake it.

'OK,' he replied.

'Getting in touch with your family?' Nicky asked, nodding at the screen. Jace didn't answer. If he thought that would block Nicky's curiosity, he was in for a big surprise.

'Chris says you're having trouble with a few things. Need any help?'

'No.'

'I hear you've got some faster kit than this back home. I told Chris he should have bought a Pentium, but he wanted a Mac and this was the best his dad could afford. What are you running?'

Chris felt a small pang of annoyance at the way his new (as of Christmas) computer was dismissed quite so easily. His father had changed jobs not long before the holiday and was now working at one of the fairly new shops in the retail park, selling home computer equipment. He'd managed to get a big discount on an Apple Mac with CD-Rom and an Internet connection, even though he hadn't been there long. Naturally, Nicky had a better, faster machine courtesy of a friend of his Uncle Fabian, but Chris wasn't the kind to be jealous over a few extra Kb of hard disk space or a 6x-speed CD-Rom drive.

Nicky wasn't exactly a techno-junkie either, but he knew enough to be able to make impressive noises about his machine, trying to get Carter to open up. And it worked.

'My dad bought me a PowerMac 7500 Christmas before last.'

'Really?' gasped Nicky, his nose well out of joint now that it was his turn to be carved up in the tech stakes.

Jace nodded. 'Yeah, it's better than a PC any day. You got Windows '95, right? Nothing there that wasn't on the Mac five years ago and the next Mac OS will blow Windows out of the water.'

The computer trilled behind him. As he turned, Chris could see that Jace had completed sending his e-mail (and there was nothing in his in-tray, worse luck). He spent a moment longer copying the files he had sent on to the floppy and then quit. Switching off the machine, he got up, tucked the disk into his shirt pocket and made room for the others.

'Thanks,' he said. 'I didn't think it would take this long.'

'Chris's modem isn't all that fast,' said Nicky. 'I've got a 14,400 speed myself . . .'

'I just upgraded to 28,800,' Jace replied automatically. 'But it doesn't make any difference if the local node's speed is slow. I can't believe CompuServe only has a 9600 modem here . . .'

'They're supposed to be upgrading in the summer,' said Chris. 'There are some faster POPs around, but it's cheaper to use the local one.' Jace nodded. There was a moment then when Chris thought maybe the ice was broken, but Jace excused himself and left the room. Nicky watched him leave with undisguised relief. He didn't like being out-scored quite so comprehensively by anyone – it didn't happen often.

'What a jerk,' said Nicky. Chris smiled secretly.

Nicky restarted the computer. After a moment or two, he sat back in the chair, drumming his fingers on the edge of the desk.

'He's wiped any copies of what he wrote,' he reported. 'He must have put the files on to that floppy he's walked off with.'

Chris had figured that out for himself. He knew there was no way to find out what Jace had been up to without that floppy.

'So, what's his big secret, I wonder?' said Nicky, who was clearly starting to become more interested in the American now that his strange behaviour was getting under his skin too.

'I don't know . . .' replied Chris. 'Maybe we're reading something into all this that isn't there.'

Nicky shot him a look that said, 'Sure, and I'm going to make a number one record with Blur.'

'Look, I'll have a word with him,' said Chris. 'Maybe he'll just tell us what his problem is.'

Nicky made a sort of snorting sound. 'Face the facts, Chris. Jace isn't going to open up to us. We'll have to start digging around for some clues.'

A light suddenly went on in his eyes. It was a sight Chris had learned to dread. Nicky loved a mystery even more than he loved football.

But the visit was only two weeks – it wasn't as if they were stuck with Jace Carter for good. Perhaps he could indulge Nicky's passion for playing detective that long. After all, it wasn't as if Jace could be involved in anything too serious.

Three

'Good plan, Nicky . . .' hissed Chris to himself, slowly backing away.

The big American lad with the earring and the zig-zag pattern cut into his short black hair was bearing down on him. Close up, he appeared to be the size of a truck and blocked out all the light in the dressing room.

Chris could hear Zak asking the huge American to calm down, but he wasn't making a big effort. In fairness, Mason Williams, the American captain, was holding his opposite number against the wall and Chris knew Zak would have made the same calculation he had – they were the only two Brits in the room with six of their 'guests'. He didn't blame Zak in the slightest for thinking that since Chris had got himself into this mess, he could deal with it himself.

Chris tried to remember just what it was he'd done to get Lowell – the hard-faced American causing the black-out – so stiffed with him. As he recalled, he'd taken Nicky's advice and asked some question about Jace Carter; Lowell had avoided giving a direct answer; Chris had offered the opinion that he thought Lowell and Jace were supposed to be mates; and then –

'Let's get one thing straight,' Lowell hissed as he came closer. 'The junkie ain't no friend of mine.'

Chris was jammed up tight against the lockers and Lowell's dark face loomed up in front of him, eclipsing everything else in the room. His eyes were like white suns, brilliant and hostile.

Chris heard a voice from somewhere behind Lowell. 'I'm not a junkie . . .' One of the six Americans was Jace himself. Chris wasn't sure if that was good news or bad.

'Shut up, Carter,' snapped another voice and there was the sound of a scuffle. Lowell didn't allow it to distract him. He remained focused on Chris (even if, that close up, Chris found it hard to focus on the American!).

'Get this straight, Stephens. We're not your room mate's buddies and we don't wanna be. So, we'd appreciate it if you kept your face out of his business and ours, OK?'

Chris got the impression that this message was as much for Carter's benefit as his. His partner's team mates were trying to isolate him and to show him that they would squash anyone who tried to interfere. He clearly wasn't very popular with any of them; the five in here were just the biggest of the bunch.

'Now, why don't you haul your Limey behind out of here and tell the coaches that we'll be out in a moment. We need to have a talk with our "team mate" in private. You hear what I'm saying?'

Lowell backed off slightly, allowing Chris to stand upright once more. He could see Zak behind Williams, looking completely bemused by all the hostility. Lowell still blocked his view of Jace, but he knew instinctively that the remaining members of the American team were crowded round him.

Well, he'd found out something at least. Jace's talent for getting on the wrong side of people wasn't confined to strangers.

Williams was patting Zak on the shoulder, apologising in a roundabout way for having hassled him, telling him that he was sure Zak understood. He stepped back, allowing Zak a clear route to the door, which the Colts captain looked happy to take.

Lowell gave Chris the same opportunity (without the apology or the friendly smile). Chris stepped into the centre of the room.

'What's all this about?' he asked Williams.

'Don't get involved, Stephens. We're offering you a way out of this.'

Good point. Chris didn't doubt that the offer wouldn't stay open that long. And after all, what did he owe Carter? The guy wasn't exactly his best friend or anything (in fact, right then, Chris wasn't sure he wouldn't have abandoned his best friend in the same circumstances – Nicky had a lot to answer for).

He took a quick look to the side, to where Jace was trapped by the entrance to the showers.

He wasn't sure what he was expecting to see, but whatever it was, Jace Carter didn't fit the bill. His three team mates were in a tight half-circle around him; two on the bench to either side, the third standing over him. He was still sitting on the bench, lacing his boots slowly. He didn't look frightened; he didn't look at all like someone about to get sorted out by his mates. In fact, he was just ignoring them.

He ignored Chris too. That was what made it so hard to just walk away. If he had been mouthing off, or even if he had been whimpering for mercy, Chris might – just might – have decided that this was a Yanks-only affair and walked away. Instead, Jace was sitting tight, toughing it out. He wasn't asking for any help at all.

Which meant Chris felt he had no choice but to give it.

He took one more step towards the door as if he was leaving and then spun round on his heel to confront Lowell and the others.

'One question,' he began, resting his hand on the door handle.

'Don't push it, Stephens,' said Williams calmly, but with enough menace in his voice to get the message across.

'It's OK, this isn't about Carter. I just wondered, why is it you guys only play girls' games?'

It took a moment for the words to penetrate Lowell's skull, then his eyes bulged with rage. 'You what?!'

'Well, over here we call baseball rounders and it's something kids and girls play. And only girls play basketball, except they call it netball.'

Even Williams, who obviously liked to hide behind his cool hard-man disguise, was looking rattled now.

'I guess you've got ice hockey and NFL, but even then, you see, you Yanks have to wear armour and stuff. Play rugby over here and they think you're a bit of a sissy if you wear a thick jersey . . .'

Lowell took a step forward, his fists clenched.

'Don't . . .' Williams commanded, but Lowell was running

pretty close to the edge of his self-control. Chris gave him a final shove.

'Is that why you guys came to play soccer over here, to develop some backbone?'

Lowell lunged at him, his big fist slashing through the air. Chris tugged at the door and pulled it towards him like a shield. He heard a sickening crunch. The door shook as if it had been struck by a train. Instantly, Chris threw his shoulder against the door and pushed it back again.

Before any of the others could react, Lowell was on the floor, nursing one hand in the other and with a healthy gash on his forehead. The three Americans clustered around Jace were all open-mouthed with amazement, as if Chris had pulled off some kind of conjuring trick.

Jace took advantage of their distraction to drive his fist into the standing guy's midriff, so that he joined Lowell on the floor, wheezing and gasping for breath. Jace leapt up through the space he had made and was alongside Chris before either of the others could move.

'I don't know what your trouble is,' Chris growled at the remaining Americans, 'but while he's staying in my house, you guys back off, get it?'

Williams stared at him coldly. Chris had him figured as a 'get you later' kind of guy.

'You just bought yourself a lot of trouble, Stephens . . .'

'I'll tell the coach how your guys slipped on the floor, shall I?' Chris said in reply, smiling.

Williams was grinning too. 'Do that. It might not be the last little accident we get round here.'

'I'll bear that in mind.'

Chris backed out of the room and along the passage, shoving Jace ahead of him towards the door that led out on to the training pitch. He didn't slow down until they were out in plain sight of all the others.

'I didn't ask for your help,' muttered Jace, his eyes glistening. Chris couldn't decide if that counted as gratitude or not. He watched Williams and the others emerge from the dressing room and report to Benton Carter. The American coach examined Lowell's cut and marched him straight back in again.

Williams was watching Chris all the time. The three guys who'd been with him spread the word round the rest of the Mount Graham team.

'No, but I may have to ask for yours later,' Chris replied.

'OK,' said Iain Walsh. 'Let's see how you guys tackle. Pair off with your partners on either side of the pitch.'

The two groups moved a little further apart. There was a great deal of whispering and pointing going on.

Once the players were lined up on opposite sides of the five-a-side pitch, Walsh told them what he wanted them to do. Each of the British players was to carry the ball across the field, round a cone and back to the start position. Their opposite numbers were to try and stop them.

He blew his whistle and everyone took off at once. A few of the Americans managed to dispossess their opponents, judging their tackles well, but the others made rash charges towards more elusive players, or were quickly dummied and passed as if they were standing still. Chris was one of those who got across both ways almost unopposed. Jace had faced off in front of him, but Chris had used his speed to go round him easily.

'OK,' called Walsh. 'Not bad.' He pointed out a couple of players to Stefan Brodenberg, who ran off to have a word with them. 'Let's try it again. Washington, Carter, Mitchell . . . try to stay mobile. Retreat in front of your man, slow him up. Don't make your tackle too early.'

That was hardly Jace's problem, Chris mused. He hadn't made any kind of attempt to tackle at all. In fact, he looked bemused by the whole manoeuvre.

Chris set off again and the result was much the same as before. Jace took a few steps back, trying to copy what he could see around him (or so it seemed to Chris), but then Chris stepped up a gear, faked left and went right, leaving his opponent tumbling on to his backside.

'Jeez, dope head, at least make an effort!' hissed Williams from the next lane. The fact that Jazz breezed past him in the next second didn't seem to make any difference to his opinion. 'Get up – tackle him!'

Chris took his time rounding the cone to give Carter time to get back on his feet. He could still hear Williams 'coaching' his team mate in a harsh, threatening whisper.

'Get him this time, Carter, or we'll get you!'

Chris went forward again, the ball at his feet, steering it a little wider to the right as he picked up the pace. He looked up and caught Williams's eye. At once, he swerved towards the American captain and ran at him. His opponent's eyes narrowed purposefully.

At the last moment, Chris flicked the ball to one side and went the other way. Jazz, who was standing watching the proceedings in amazement, played an instinctive return pass. Williams was left floundering hopelessly as Chris picked up the ball again without breaking stride and pulled the ball under the sole of his boot as he came to a stop.

Before he had time to congratulate himself, though, he heard a rush of feet and he was sent crashing down to the ground. He took most of the impact on his arm and shoulder, but he still hit the unforgiving surface of the all-weather pitch hard enough to bounce.

There was a collective gasp from the onlookers, then a shrill blast on a whistle. Chris became aware that Walsh was bending over him, cradling his head.

'Are you OK?'

'Never mind me, did I damage the floor?' quipped Chris. He was shaken, but not too badly hurt. His shoulder felt banged about, but there were no broken bones as far as he could tell.

Walsh helped him to his feet. 'Come over to the sidelines. I'll have the club doctor take a squint at you.'

Chris allowed himself to be guided to the touchline. He felt a little light-headed, but there was no pain.

'I'm OK, honest. Just give me a minute to get myself together.'

By the time he was sitting on the bench and a physio had wiped him over with a sponge, Chris was already feeling better. He'd taken worse tackles than that and survived – but never one so unexpected.

Iain Walsh, meanwhile, had gone back on to the pitch to confront the perpetrator.

'What are you playing at?' he roared.

Carter took a step backwards in the face of the tirade. He looked genuinely surprised. There were plenty of other bemused faces in the ring of players around him, too.

'I thought I was supposed to tackle him . . .' Jace answered lamely.

'Tackle him, yes! No-one said anything about assaulting him! This is just a training exercise, for heaven's sake. What were you thinking of?'

Jace didn't answer. He looked very pale and confused. He looked around at his countrymen for support, but there was none there. A couple of the Colts had been all ready to go steaming in, looking for revenge, but were put off by Walsh's quick reactions.

'Chris saves his neck and this is how he gets repaid?' muttered Mac. Players from both teams nodded their heads in agreement.

'Get off,' said Walsh, gesturing towards the changing rooms. 'I'll speak with Stefan about you later.'

'There's no need,' said Chris.

Walsh turned round. Chris was heading over towards them looking the worse for wear.

'You can't blame Jace . . . he just over-reacted. I was taking the Michael out of his captain and he got mad. It's my fault.'

'That's not the point –' Walsh began.

'Look, I'm OK,' said Chris. 'Let's just forget it, huh?'

Walsh knew Chris well enough to know that he didn't hold a grudge for long, but he was amazed to see Chris quite so happy to accept being slammed to the ground. At the same time, the last thing he wanted was to divide the two teams into bitter enemies.

'Are you sure?'

'Yeah,' said Chris, stretching out his hand to take hold of Jace's. He shook it warmly and looked round to make sure that everyone was looking. 'See? No bad feelings.'

No-one reacted much as they watched Chris make such a public job of reconciliation. A few of the Colts raised their eyebrows as if to say that they thought Chris must have banged his head when he landed; the Americans all remained perfectly still, rigidly controlling their emotions. At the centre of the circle, Chris put his arm round Jace's shoulder.

'Come on, let's you and me go over here and work on that routine without getting in anyone else's way.' He rolled a ball out from under his boot and steered Jace into following it. They quickly put ten metres between themselves and the others. Chris bent slowly and picked up the ball, coming face to face with Jace, but looking past him as Walsh finally shook his head and restarted the practice.

Moments later, the others were engaged in their drills once more. There was a familiar background of shouting and the patter of footballs skipping over the tarmac. Chris knew that everyone was still watching them from the corner of their eyes, but he was far enough away and on the fringes of their attention to be able to deal with Jace without interruption.

'I'm genuinely sorry –' Jace began.

'I'll talk, you listen,' Chris replied sharply. 'I'm about to start asking you some questions and you better give me some answers, or I'll wrap you up in a parcel and air mail you back to the States. Or I'll just invite your team mates over and lock you in a room with them.'

Chris tried to keep his body relaxed and his face smiling, so that no-one would suspect what was going on. There was no mistaking the violence in his voice, though. Jace dropped his chin on to his chest.

'OK. Question one. You've never played football in your life before, have you?'

Jace lifted his head quickly. 'I have –' he protested, though his eyes had defeat written large in them.

'I'm not talking about kicking a ball around the park with some of your mates,' Chris jumped in. 'I'm talking about organised games. Real football. You don't play for the school at all, do you?'

Jace hesitated for a moment longer and then shook his head.

'So, what were we playing back there? American football?'

This time the other boy nodded. 'I play line-backer at school.'

Chris had recorded enough late-night Channel 4 on Mondays to know what that meant. Line-backers were the guys who slammed themselves into running backs. By his standards, Jace had enacted a perfect tackle on Chris. Even wearing padding and a helmet, Chris thought he would still have been rattled by that hit.

'OK. Good start,' said Chris. 'Question two. If you're not part of the soccer team, what are you doing here?'

He saw a small twitch in Jace's eyes as he trotted out the answer. 'My cousin was supposed to come, but he got sick the day before the flight. No-one else could make it at the last moment and it didn't make sense to waste the ticket, so Uncle Benford said I could come in his place.'

That sounded plausible, but it also sounded well rehearsed.

'I might just buy that,' Chris continued, with his fake smile still in place (he caught Walsh watching them carefully), 'except for the secrecy. You've been lying since you first got here.'

'No I haven't!' protested Jace. 'I just didn't tell you the truth!'

'Like there's a difference,' scoffed Chris. As he said it, the image popped into his mind of all the times he had not lied/not told his father something. It was like the good angel in a comic strip, reminding him not to be such a hypocrite.

This is different, the bad angel replied in his mind. And he could just about convince himself that it was true.

'So, why'd you come?' he asked.

'I told you –'

Chris cut him off again. 'I heard all that guff about your sick cousin; that's not what I'm asking. I want to know why you *wanted* to come.'

Chris could see Jace struggling with the answer. Like a shark smelling blood, he moved in closer.

'This is a soccer exchange, Jace. It's not like you've scored a free holiday. There's not that much time to play tourist – and when you had your chance on Monday, you couldn't have been less interested! So, if you don't play football and you don't really like it, why bother coming?'

Chris flicked the ball back and forward along his arm, making a small effort to appear as if he was talking to Jace about football. The pretence was wasted, however. Anyone a mile away could have seen that Jace was close to panic, groping for an answer to the question, his mouth flapping like a stranded fish.

'I can't!' Jace whimpered after a few more seconds.

'What?' asked Chris.

'I can't tell you!'

Chris let the ball fall to the ground, whirled round and fired a volley against the fence. The ball flashed into the wiring like a missile and there was a crash like a dustbin lid free-falling on to concrete.

'Suit yourself,' said Chris. 'It's not like it's really my business, and it's not like I give a damn. But for the next two weeks you're living with me, and judging by the way your mates are looking at you, I'd bet I'm just about the only friend you've got.'

He moved away and collected the ball, taking a moment to get his temper back under control. By the time he got back, Jace had recovered as well, and his defences were back up. Chris tossed him the ball.

'What am I supposed to do with this?' he asked.

'There's still an hour of practice left,' said Chris. 'And now it's my turn to tackle you.'

Four

Chris didn't say anything to anyone else about the conversation with Jace until he met up with Nicky on Wednesday evening. The practice sessions went off OK, if you didn't count the obvious tension between the two teams in the dressing rooms. Guessing that something was up, the United coaching staff, Walsh, Sean Priest, Mr Carter and Stefan all kept a wary eye on the boys while they were together. Of course, once everyone split up into their pairs in the evening, no-one had any control over the situation at all.

From what Chris could tell from snatched conversations with Mac and Jazz, the incident in the dressing room had threatened to divide the two teams into warring factions, but the spectacle of Jace trashing Chris on the training pitch had left everyone confused. It was becoming clear to everyone that the other Americans had little time for Jace Carter, but no-one seemed very clear any more about whether or not that meant the Brits should hate all the Yanks, whose side Jace was on, or what Chris was doing in the middle of it all anyway.

Over the two days, Chris made a conscious effort to try and get inside Jace's guard. He made a big show of helping Jace with the training sessions and sitting with him at lunchtime. Whenever anyone else was around, Chris made it very plain that if you wanted to mess with Jace, you'd have to do it through him. The Yanks, consequently, were keeping their distance.

When they were alone, though, Chris kept needling at Jace, demanding that he tell the truth about himself. With every hour, Chris became less and less happy about having Jace in the same house while he was keeping his secrets locked up.

'So, what has he had to say for himself?' asked Nicky.

They were standing in the queue at the hamburger stall. As always on a Wednesday, Nicky had had early evening practice with Gainsbury Town, rivals of the Colts in the Oldcester District Youth League. He'd had to rush back in order to meet up with Chris and his father in town. When he'd been reminded that they had Jace for extra company at the evening game, he'd scowled heavily.

The queue wasn't too long, which was good in one way because Nicky was starving, but it meant they didn't have long to compare notes about the two days since Nicky had last seen Jace. Chris got him up to date rapidly.

'I don't suppose you've seen any replies to his e-mail?' Nicky asked.

Chris hadn't and he felt really guilty about having even tried.

'I'm not sure about snooping into private stuff, Nicky. It'd be like searching his room.'

'That's a good idea too.'

'Nicky!'

'What?' cried Nicky, his face a picture of wounded innocence. He brushed away a lock of his black hair the wind had dragged over his eyes and shuffled forward as the queue moved up a place.

'I just think we're jumping to conclusions,' Chris replied at last, trying to keep his voice calm. He could sense that Nicky was about to dive off at the deep end. 'Remember the last time.'

'That business with Russell Jones was completely different,' Nicky complained.

'How? We thought Russell had something to hide; he did. We thought he was a crook; he wasn't.' At least, he wasn't *the crook*, which was the important issue.

Nicky replied with a sarcastic smile and a wave of his hands that almost knocked a pile of hot dogs out of the arms of a large, black-haired bloke in glasses. The bloke growled at Nicky.

'What's the matter with you, Sumo?' snapped Nicky instantly.

The bloke looked as if he was prepared to strangle Nicky,

but that was going to be difficult with a dozen hot dogs balanced on his hands. He skulked off, complaining to the other people in the queue about rude kids who ought to be at home instead of getting under the feet of real fans.

Chris sighed, aware that several other people were now watching him and Nicky as if they were a pair of delinquents caught spraying graffiti on the town hall. Nicky obviously wasn't aware of this at all and continued to examine the Jace problem in the little time they had before they reached the front of the queue.

'Look, I know what you're saying about Russell. We had him wrong. He's an all right bloke and a good goalkeeper. But there was something suss about him and we found out the truth.'

'And in the process, I got kidnapped and the university sports pavilion got burned down.'

'It was a dump anyway . . .' sighed Nicky. 'You're missing the point. Things turned out OK in the end, right? And if we hadn't got involved, Russell would still be stuck with his brother and all the stuff that got nicked would never have been found.' Nicky drifted off for a moment, remembering the day they had been at Star Park, about to watch a game, only to be called up to the executive box for a special celebration to mark the safe return of Sean Priest's memorabilia, now on display in the club museum. 'We were heroes,' he added.

Chris's memories featured more on spending three days tied up and gagged after being abducted by Russell's maniac of a brother. It was clear he and Nicky weren't going to see eye to eye on this one.

'So how is that the same as this stuff with Jace?'

Nicky rolled his eyes up as if he was amazed that Chris couldn't see the obvious. 'Don't you get it?' He lifted his hand so that he could start counting points off on his fingers, something he only did when he felt Chris was being too thick to understand.

One finger. 'Jace isn't part of the football team, but he comes on the exchange. Why? Because his uncle is the school principal, or whatever they call their head teachers over there.'

Two. 'The other kids from the school all hate him. Why?'

'Because he's the head's nephew?' offered Chris, feeling that he ought to contribute.

'Hardly,' said Nicky. 'They don't seem so down on this other bloke, Stafford –'

'Stockton.'

'Whatever. And he's the head's son, right?'

It was a fair point. Chris tried to think of another reason for Jace's clear and conspicuous unpopularity.

'OK. Maybe this Stockton character is everybody's mate, and they don't like it that Jace has taken his place.'

Once again, Nicky shook his head. 'Can't be. I mean, if Stock Cupboard's ill and can't come, that's not Jace's fault, right? No, it has to go deeper than that . . .'

Chris could tell that Nicky had already reached a conclusion. Realising he might as well get it over with, he shrugged and asked Nicky what he thought Jace's problem was.

Three. 'Drugs!'

Nicky uttered that one word in a voice that was meant to be close to a whisper, but which carried so much certainty and conviction that everyone around them in the queue heard it. Chris jumped, startled by it. He took a rapid look around – they were now the focus of attention of about twelve people. Chris gave them a sickly smile as he caught them looking at him. He also saw a police constable who was – mercifully – just out of hearing range.

'Nicky!' he hissed under his breath.

Oblivious to all around him, Nicky was already developing point three, his eyes focused off into the distance, where the whole plot was as clear as a bell to him.

'Think about it. What were those names the other guys called him? Dope-head? And what's all this business with secret e-mail messages?'

Chris closed his eyes and wished he could teleport back to his seat in the Easter Road Stand. Or anywhere rather than here. Nicky was smiling with the certainty of someone who could not only see the wood for the trees, but who had a big axe and a chainsaw to help him improve the view.

'For goodness sake, Nicky . . .' he sighed urgently. The queue shuffled further forward; there was just one customer in front of them now.

'Maybe he's a messenger, here to contact someone. Or –'

'Give up, Nicky!' Chris exploded (by then, it hardly mattered if he drew any more attention to them; several people in the queue were actually pushing closer so they could catch more of what was being said). 'Do you honestly think Jace looks some kind of criminal mastermind?'

Nicky shrugged in a way that suggested he was prepared to continue to think the same way whatever Chris believed.

Chris was on the point of explaining just why Nicky was being ridiculous (even though he had as little proof that Jace was innocent as Nicky had that he was guilty) when the constable appeared alongside them.

'Now then, lads, let's have a little less fuss.'

Nicky looked up at the copper with some surprise. The consequences of his outburst hadn't occurred to him even yet. 'What's wrong? We haven't done anything!'

Chris fancied he could hear a few of the adults round them muttering about 'young lads today' and 'no respect for their elders'. He waited for one of them to actually accuse him of knowing a foreign criminal.

'Just calm down, OK?' the policeman demanded.

Nicky twitched his mouth, but he was saved from answering when the man in front of them walked off with a hot dog clamped between his teeth. He turned away from the policeman and looked up at the guy in the fast food stall.

'A hot dog, a burger and fries and –'

'You'll have to wait for the hot dogs,' the fast food man broke in, sounding tired and harassed.

'What?'

'That gentleman just had the last one. I'm getting some more ready; it'll be about ten minutes, OK?'

Nicky's face grew darker. He glowered at the customer who had just walked away, but his mind had already worked out that the real culprit had been the large bloke with the black hair.

'Sure; I'll miss the whole first half, shall I, waiting for you? No problem.'

There were some impatient growls from behind them. Chris made up his mind that he wasn't hungry.

'Do you want something else?' asked the fast food man.

'That depends,' asked Nicky. 'Any chance of a burger by the end of the season?'

The fast food man had clearly lived too long behind that counter to be offended by the fast lip of someone Nicky's size. He folded his arms and waited, knowing that the growing rumble of the people stuck in the queue behind Nicky would move things along faster than he ever could.

'Why don't you order your food, son, and then button your lip,' said the policeman. There were murmurs of agreement from the queue. It was the first time Chris could ever remember a copper being congratulated on his work at a football match.

Nicky opened his mouth to add some more fuel to the fire (Chris had a momentary flash of a tour of the police custody facilities on the other side of the ground) when a new voice intruded on the proceedings.

'It's OK, officer, I'll take care of these two.'

A few of the spectators recognised Sean Priest from his time playing for United. The policeman looked relieved when he saw the official pass Priest was wearing on his lapel.

'They're all yours,' he said.

Priest walked the remaining few feet over to where Chris and Nicky were standing, turning them away from the burger bar and back towards the centre of the walkway under the stand.

'My burger!' howled Nicky.

'We'll eat later,' said Sean. 'I need a word with you two.'

They walked through the throng of people making their way to their seats, and headed towards a door marked 'PRIVATE'.

'Are you here with your dad?' asked Priest.

'Yes,' Chris replied. And then, remembering, he added: 'And Jace Carter is with us too.'

Priest's mouth turned up in a small smile. He waved towards one of the stewards, told him the seat numbers where Mr Stephens and Jace would be sitting, and asked him to take them 'upstairs'.

Nicky was beaming now. He had developed quite a liking for the posh life and the view from the boxes was as good as you could find anywhere in the ground.

'I wonder if they'll give us anything to eat, like last time,' he whispered to Chris, grinning broadly. Chris doubted it; the last time Priest had taken them 'upstairs' they were the heroes of the hour, not hooligans to be rescued from a near riot in front of a burger bar.

Still, it did look as if Nicky might be right. They climbed what felt like several hundred concrete steps up inside the stand, and came out through an unmarked door on to a carpeted landing. Sean led them towards a door on the other side of the passage, opening it and groping for the light. He held the door open and ushered them in.

It was one of the executive boxes, but empty. No smiling directors and company managers swilling champagne and eating piles of food; no waiters in smart uniforms to fetch Coke or sandwiches; even the heating was off. Nicky's face became very grumpy.

'Take a seat,' said Priest. 'We can have a quick word in here without anyone overhearing, and if the game starts, we won't miss anything.'

He looked at his watch. It was about 7.25. Both the teams were out on the pitch, far below. United's red and blue were at the River End, with Star Park's most fanatical supporters at their backs. Up here, it was almost difficult to hear them.

Priest dropped into one of the comfortable armchairs in the middle of the room, facing the large window that looked down on the pitch. The two boys chose seats on his left. Chris had left a seat between himself and Priest, but Nicky didn't fall for that and actually sat on one further along.

If Priest noticed they were keeping their distance, he didn't say anything. Instead, he unfastened his coat, stretched out and pulled a programme from his pocket as if he was going to read it.

'So, Chris, how are you getting on with Jace Carter?'

It was hardly a surprise that this was what he wanted to talk about. After all, it had been pretty obvious to all concerned that the two teams weren't getting along like a house on fire, or even a house with its central heating on. Priest had been at most of the training sessions and he must have been able to see that there was a great deal of friction. Plus, Iain Walsh would have reported to him by now, and Walsh *definitely* knew that something was amiss. Chris wondered if Priest knew about the infamous tackle incident.

'I don't know . . . OK, I guess,' he said, knowing how lame it sounded.

To his surprise, all Priest said was: 'Good.' It even sounded as though he meant it.

Chris tried to relax a little more and stole a quick glance at Nicky, who was staring up at the ceiling.

'Has he seen much of the other Americans while he's been at your house?'

That sounded like a question that could be answered more truthfully.

'No, not really. His uncle came over last night for an hour, but that's all.' In the silence that followed, he looked round at Nicky again, to find his friend poking around in the ash tray on the arm of the chair.

That seemed to prove once and for all that he couldn't expect any help from Fiorentini.

Priest leafed through his programme and looked out of the window into the glare of the floodlights.

'Do you think that he has any particular friends among the other Yanks?' he asked.

This was beginning to drive Chris mad. Surely Priest knew the score? Once again, he took a brief glance in Nicky's direction, hoping for a little help, but Nicky was now making a very close study of the front of his jacket and he didn't even look up when Chris tried to jab him with his elbow.

'Actually –' Chris began as he turned back, resigned to having to come clean.

'The truth is,' Priest said, having started at the same moment, 'I think Jace is a bit of an outsider. He's had some problems at home and the other guys seem to resent the fact that he's come on this trip.'

Chris tried to think of a tactful way to ask why Jace had been picked as the last-minute substitute. The best he could come up with was: 'Was there someone else they'd have preferred to come instead?'

Priest shook his head. 'Not that I know of. Mr Carter hasn't said anything like that to me. No, I think it's just that they don't really get on with Jace.'

Chris tried to work out if Priest knew more than he was saying, but he got nowhere. The youth team manager was leaning forward now, looking down on to the pitch where Notts County were preparing to kick off. At that moment, the door opened and the steward put his head round the door.

'They're in the directors' enclosure, Sean – Row D.'

Priest thanked the man and stood up. 'Come on, let's go and join them.'

Nicky rose quickly, clearly happy at the prospect of getting out. Chris followed suit and the three of them walked towards the door. In the background, Chris heard the shrill blast of the ref's whistle.

'Look,' said Priest, stopping suddenly. 'I don't want you to miss the game, but I just want to tell you this. It would be a personal favour to me if you'd keep an eye on Jace a bit. He could do with a friend, so just give the guy a chance, OK? Whatever you've heard about him, it's not true.'

It's not just what we've been told, Chris thought, it's what we've found out for ourselves. He kept that fact to himself and just nodded.

'Great,' said Priest, smiling. 'What about you, Fiorentini? Have you got anything you want to say?'

'Yeah,' replied Nicky. 'Can we get something to eat? I'm starving!'

Five

'Have you got a minute?' said Chris. 'I'd like to talk.'

Jace looked up and met Chris's enquiry with his normal silence. He had just walked into the kitchen, carrying a small yellow and black canister which Chris recognised as a Kodak film. He put it on the shelf beside the coffee jar and took down the sugar to make himself some breakfast.

It was 8.30am. In about 30 minutes, Mac's father would be arriving to drive them over to the practice ground on London Road for another morning of coaching. In the afternoon, the whole group was going to go ten-pin bowling. To round off the day, a disco had been organised at Spirebrook Comp in the evening, to which the Americans had been invited.

Chris was looking forward to all of it. The exchange visit (or this half, at least) was supposed to be for the benefit of the Americans, but the Colts were getting some excellent coaching from Priest's staff at Oldcester United, alongside the regular youth team players and some other visitors. The Colts had played a short game on Wednesday afternoon against United's Under-15s, and had taken a 3–0 beating, but Chris had loved every minute of it.

At the end of the two weeks, he knew, Priest had organised a four-way mini-league to complete the Americans' stay. On Friday and Saturday, Mount Graham and the Colts would be pitched against the United youth squad and a team from Rotterdam FC in Holland – the club where Priest had finished his playing career. There was even talk of a trophy for the winners.

At the moment, though, that all seemed a long way away. Chris had tried to think how he was going to turn round the situation with his house guest as Priest had asked. The way

Jace clammed up the moment you spoke to him, it wasn't going to be easy.

Chris's father had just left for work; that meant he had a few minutes alone with Jace to see if he could make any progress.

'Can it wait?' asked Jace. 'I want to see if I've had any e-mail.'

He'd checked it last night when they'd got back from the football; Chris gathered there hadn't been anything for Jace, just a message for Chris from the guys he was working on the Web page with, urging him to get his bit finished.

Jace crammed a slice of toast into his mouth (it had peanut butter *and* jam on – jelly as Jace called it; how could he eat that stuff together?) and made as if to walk past Chris. Chris got up from his stool quickly and beat him through the door.

'We'll talk while you look,' he said.

Jace stopped in the kitchen doorway.

'This stuff is private,' he said in a hostile, prickly way.

Chris wasn't going to be put off. 'So turn the screen away. Mac will be here soon and I want to get this done now.'

They went upstairs. Or rather, Chris went upstairs and Jace followed a minute or so later, obviously realising that Chris wasn't going to give way over this. He went to fetch the floppy disk from his room while Chris started up and logged on to CompuServe. There were a couple of messages waiting.

Jace arrived just as he was preparing to pull the incoming mail into the in-basket.

'Hey!' he cried, seeing what Chris was doing. 'I said this stuff was private!'

'I'm not going to read it!' Chris snapped back.

'I don't want you even seeing who might be replying,' Jace insisted.

Chris released the mouse and folded his arms, but didn't give up his seat. 'Jace, get real. This is my bedroom. I could log on any time I wanted and look at what I wanted and you'd never know.' He knew that Jace had considered the possibility, but that he was desperate enough to realise he had no choice but to trust Chris that far. 'Besides, did it never occur to you that *I* might have private stuff coming in that I don't want *you* to see?'

Jace looked as if he wanted to argue. Chris remained defiantly in his chair. It was a perfect stand-off.

The doorbell rang.

'Damn,' muttered Chris. He thought about ignoring it but decided he couldn't. 'This'll keep,' he told Jace, and swept out of the room. He heard Jace leap into his chair before he had even reached the top of the stairs.

Continuing to curse Jace's good luck as he stamped down the stairs, Chris walked up to the front door, expecting to find the milkman standing there asking for payment or the postman struggling with a packet that wouldn't fit through the letter box. It was neither.

The man at the door was a tall guy with neatly cut blond hair, a square, weathered kind of face and narrow eyes with pale irises. He wasn't that tall, but he was pretty stocky. He was dressed in a plain, navy mackintosh, belted against the coolness of the morning, plus gloves and a scarf. He wasn't looking through the glass into the house, but stood to one side, hands crossed in front of him, staring neutrally at the brickwork opposite.

Spirebrook wasn't some inner-city estate with burglaries every five minutes – well, not all of Spirebrook was, anyway – but Chris's father always made sure Chris slipped the chain on to the door when he left him alone in the house. Chris opened the door as far as it would go and bent his head to speak into the gap.

'Yes?'

The man only turned to face him once Chris had spoken, as if he was only aware Chris was there when he heard his voice. He smiled in a friendly fashion and bent down slightly as he replied.

'Good morning. Are you Chris Stephens?'

Was that an American accent? Chris's curiosity was piqued at once.

'Yes,' he replied cautiously (though not as cautiously as his father would have preferred; the idea was that Chris was supposed to ask questions about strangers appearing at the door, not answer them).

'Great!' the man replied brightly. 'My name is Ripley and I'm with the US Consulate in London. You know what that is?'

Barely. Chris nodded anyway.

'We look after American nationals while they're in your country, that kind of thing,' the man explained. He lowered his voice a little, then added: 'I understand you have one of my countrymen staying with you now.'

Chris opened his mouth to answer, then closed it again. He had no reason to mistrust the man, but his father had ingrained some very cautious habits in him and he wasn't about to abandon them completely.

Ripley smiled, as if he wanted to show that he wasn't offended by Chris's defensiveness.

'Jace Goodman? He's over here on a soccer exchange?'

Once again, Chris made as if he was going to say something, but choked on it. What had Ripley called Jace? Goodman? That was a curious error for a government official to make.

Chris managed to find a way to stall for time.

'Do you have any ID?'

Ripley's friendly smile became even broader. He reached inside his mac, struggling to reach a pocket in there.

'I can see you're a smart boy. It always pays to be careful,' he said, pulling out a wallet and flicking it open. Inside, there was a plastic identity card, with 'US GOVERNMENT' on the top, a picture of Ripley underneath, and various numbers and logos and other official-looking stuff all round. It looked OK.

'What's all this about?' asked Chris.

'I have some news for Jace – family problems back home,' Ripley replied, snapping the wallet shut. 'It's nothing really serious, but I need to talk to him. Is he in?'

Chris nodded automatically. He noticed Ripley had a long scar along the line of his jaw. He looked at it curiously.

Ripley waited for a moment to see if Chris was prepared to open the door. When he realised that he wasn't, he added, 'Actually, Jace could be in a spot of trouble. His father was arrested back home in the States. Jace might be involved somehow. I really need to speak with him and find out what he knows.'

So, Nicky was half-right at least!

'Have you come to arrest him?' Chris asked.

'Good lord, no!' the man laughed. 'I don't have any authority to do that here in the UK. I'd need your British police to help me if that was what I wanted! Don't worry, I'm not going to take Jace anywhere, I just need to have a talk with him.'

Chris nodded. He pictured Jace upstairs, retrieving his secret messages on the computer. Maybe he already knew that his father had been arrested? Maybe he was hiding evidence in his room?

'Could I come in now?' Ripley asked, breaking in on Chris's train of thought. 'I'm from California and I still haven't got used to your climate!'

Chris checked his watch. In less than twenty minutes, Mac's father would arrive. Chris was pretty sure he wouldn't be murdered or robbed in just twenty minutes, so he closed the door and slipped the chain. He was still a little nervous about breaking the rules his father had drummed into him, but Ripley was putting his wallet back into the inside pocket it had come from and he didn't seem at all threatening.

Chris opened the door.

To his relief, Ripley didn't come through the door like somebody out of *NYPD Blue*, but stepped into the hall, unbelting his raincoat to reveal a very smart suit in a kind of light, earthy brown. Chris turned away and walked towards the stairs, preparing to call Jace. He jumped when Ripley laid a hand on his shoulder.

'Just ask him to come down,' whispered Ripley, taking off his gloves. 'No need to spook the boy.'

Chris nodded, and turned back to look up the stairs. 'Jace?'

They both stood there, waiting. Chris offered Ripley a nervous grin.

'Jace!' he called again, with a little bit more urgency and volume. Still there was silence.

Suddenly, Ripley was pushing past him.

'Stay here!' he commanded, climbing the stairs two at a time. Chris obeyed that instruction for as long as it took for Ripley to reach the landing, then ran up behind him.

Ripley had gone straight to Chris's room at the front of the house and was on his way back out as Chris arrived. He ignored Chris completely, ducking his head round the door of Chris's father's room to take a peek in there and then heading for the back of the house.

Jace wasn't in the spare bedroom, and when Ripley opened the bathroom door, Chris saw that the window was wide open, the breeze snatching at the curtains. Ripley glared at Chris; he didn't need to ask whether this was something Chris expected to see. He looked out of the window. Chris knew that he would be able to see the roof of the kitchen extension just below, and then the garden stretching towards some hedges at the bottom.

Ripley looked less than pleased to find Jace gone. He looked at Chris again, his expression bleak with annoyance, then returned to the back bedroom. Chris stepped forward to take a cautious peek through the door; Ripley was emptying the drawers on to the floor, kicking through Jace's clothes. He looked through the cases on top of the wardrobe, searched jacket and jeans pockets, and checked under the bed. It took less than two minutes.

'What was he doing before I called?' demanded Ripley, with no trace of a smile now.

'Nothing!' Chris lied automatically, but his eyes flickered towards the front bedroom. Ripley pushed past and went to Chris's room again.

The computer screen showed the in-basket of his CompuServe software. There were a couple of e-mail messages for Chris; nothing else.

'Did he get any mail this morning?' asked Ripley, hurriedly.

'I don't know,' replied Chris honestly. 'It doesn't look like it.'

'Maybe he deleted the file,' said Ripley.

'I doubt it,' said Chris. 'He didn't even have time to log off.' Chris bent over the keyboard and disconnected the line. There was no sign of Jace's floppy disk, either in the drive or on the desk.

Jace hadn't even had time to go to his room and get his jacket, but he'd made sure he had the disk with him when he disappeared out the bathroom window.

Ripley looked around, frustrated and angry. He banged one fist into his other palm and cursed loudly. Chris noticed he had a heavy signet ring on his right hand. While he was looking at that, Ripley was fixing his gaze on Chris.

'Guess this proves Goodman is involved, eh?' he said. He didn't wait for an answer. 'Listen, I'm going to see if I can track him down. If he comes back here, try and get him to hang around.'

'Should I phone you or anything?' Chris asked.

'Better not,' Ripley replied grimly. 'I'll contact you.'

Chris nodded. Ripley left the room, running swiftly down the stairs. Chris heard the front door close.

The episode had concluded so quickly that Chris was left standing in front of the computer, wondering what to make of it all. He walked through to the bathroom and looked out over the garden, wondering if he would catch sight of Jace anywhere. The garden was flanked on either side by their neighbours and backed on to a similar garden on the next road along. An old apple tree at the foot of the garden would have provided one way for Jace to slip over the fence once he had made his way down from the roof of the kitchen, or he could have dropped directly down on to the driveway next door.

Chris pulled the curtain back inside and closed the window, making sure it was secure. Leaving the bathroom, he took a moment to survey the mess in Jace's room, deciding that it wasn't down to him to clear it up. It was just starting to dawn on Chris that he was going to have a lot of explaining to do if people knew Jace had run off.

Would he come back? Chris had no idea. He suspected not, now that Jace believed his hiding place had been rumbled. Chris guessed he must have heard him talking to Ripley at the door, figured out who it was, and fled the moment he realised that he was opening the door.

It would have been a close-run thing. He must have slipped into the bathroom just as Ripley was about to set foot on to the stairs. No time to grab anything – except the floppy disk. If he had left it another second or two, Ripley would have seen him slip out through the window, or caught him on the kitchen roof.

Chris paused, thinking this through. He stared through the open door of his room, looking at the computer. The CompuServe in-tray was empty. It only took a moment to delete a file from there, assuming there had been anything to delete in the first place. Had Jace read something quickly and then trashed it? Chris pondered that for a moment longer. Jace seemed to want to keep a copy of stuff on the floppy. Had he managed to squeeze out enough time to do that?

Chris doubted it. Which made him wonder if Jace hadn't deleted any incoming e-mail, but just hidden it quickly so that he could look at it again later. It was as quick to move a file on the Mac as it was to delete one.

It could have been hidden anywhere in the maze of files and folders Chris had on his hard drive, but Chris figured it would have to be somewhere accessible, somewhere where Jace could have just dragged the file quickly before he fled from the room.

Chris took his seat in front of the Mac. Using the computer's 'Find' option, he got it to search his hard drive for any file created that day. In just a second, it had tracked down an incoming e-mail message to the system folder.

Looking at the icon on his screen, Chris hesitated for a moment. Was he prepared to go poking around in Jace's affairs? What right did he have? Of course, it did now look as if Nicky was right and Jace was involved somehow in something illegal, but Chris still couldn't convince himself that this meant he could sneak a look at some private correspondence.

In the end, he made a compromise with himself. He duplicated the file and hid it in a private folder of his own. That way he could make up his mind later . . .

Moments later, the doorbell rang again. This time, Chris shut down the computer before he went downstairs. It was Mac, bouncing up and down on the doorstep, urging him to hurry. Chris could see Mr MacIntyre's car outside, the engine running.

They were waiting to take him and Jace to the practice. Chris took a long deep breath and opened the door.

⚽

'You must have some idea where he went!' cried Mr Carter.

'I'm sorry,' said Chris. 'I don't.'

Benford Carter shot Priest a worried look. Chris watched them both, trying to work out how much they knew already and how much more he should tell them.

Or not tell them. Chris was feeling pretty guilty. He'd been lying all morning, partly because he was confused about what he was supposed to do and partly because if Ripley was right about Jace's 'family', then Benford Carter, his uncle, might be a suspect too.

'Do you think he went to meet someone?' Priest asked him.

'I don't think so,' said Chris. He could be pretty confident of that. In fact, Jace had been deliberately trying *not* to meet someone, though Chris kept that fact to himself for now.

'It's not very likely,' moaned Mr Carter. 'Who does he know in Oldcester, England? Just the guys in the two teams, and they're all here.'

'I know,' said Priest. 'That's what makes it so strange that he's just run off.'

The two men thought it through some more.

'Do you think he's just run off to avoid the morning practice?' Priest offered. 'It's no secret he hasn't been doing too well . . .' Benford shot him a warning glance. Priest shook his head.

'Don't worry, Benford. I think Chris has figured out by now that Jace isn't part of the Mount Graham soccer team.'

That information didn't seem to cheer Mr Carter up at all. He looked at Chris in a despairing way, and then turned away to pace up and down, following a short figure of eight on the parking space.

Chris looked across the field. The others were already starting the day's coaching session. He could hear them shouting encouragement to each other as they lapped the pitch, running short sprints behind the goalmouths.

'This whole thing is starting to come apart,' Mr Carter said sorrowfully.

'Maybe not,' said Priest. 'This doesn't have to be anything sinister. It really could be that Jace is just bunking off practice. Maybe he's had enough of the other guys giving him a hard time.'

That was closer to the kind of thing Benford Carter needed to hear. He put on a brave smile as he walked back towards them. 'You think so?'

'Maybe,' said Priest. 'He'll either turn up here or at Chris's place. Seemed to me he was quite looking forward to going bowling.'

Mr Carter had gained the same impression. 'You're right, of course. We'll just wait, at least for now. Perhaps someone should let Chris's father know . . .?'

'He's not at home today,' Chris blurted out quickly. 'He's at work. I'll wait at home to see if Jace turns up, if you like.'

'Are you sure?' asked Priest.

Chris nodded. Anything was better than his father finding out that he had allowed their house guest to be scared into fleeing out of the bathroom window (a detail of Jace's absence Chris hadn't told anyone as yet).

'It's going to be funny at practice without a partner anyway. As soon as he turns up, I'll call your mobile and someone can come pick us up.'

That was a sensible solution and Priest nodded thankfully. 'I'll take you home,' he said. Chris felt a wave of relief. If he could get Priest on his own, perhaps he could tell him some more of the details.

'No,' interrupted Benford Carter. 'You have work to do here. I'll take him.'

Uh oh, Chris thought.

There wasn't any clever way to get out of this, so he allowed himself to be steered to the passenger seat of the Ford Orion Carter had hired. Priest waved, then turned to run over to the practice field.

'You'll have to give me directions,' said Benford. 'I still haven't got used to your city. Back home, all the streets run in straight lines – I can't cope with the way yours wander all over the place!'

Chris started to navigate, getting Benford to turn right on to London Road – which the American managed with a little difficulty – then leading him on to the ring road, which was the most convenient way to show him, even if not quite the shortest.

Waiting at a set of traffic lights, Mr Carter turned to Chris (not easy, since his large body was held tight by the seatbelt) and asked: 'You will call as soon as Jace appears, won't you?'

'Yes,' Chris replied. He managed to change the subject by pointing through the windscreen. 'Follow the signs for the university.'

He watched Mr Carter as they tip-toed nervously round

a mini-roundabout towards the turning for Spirebrook, which lay between the ring road and the river. He appeared genuinely worried, although it was impossible to tell whether this was for Jace's safety, or because he thought the family criminal conspiracy was about to unravel (or because he was about to ram the Orion into the back of a lorry). The more Chris considered it, though, the less he could think of Benford Carter as being involved in anything that would be big enough to cause a federal agent to come all the way to Britain.

In his heart, he felt the same about Jace.

He desperately wanted to know more so that he could put the pieces of the puzzle together. Perhaps this journey with Mr Carter wasn't such a bad idea after all.

'Mr Carter, who are Jace's parents?'

Once out, the question sounded a bit blunter than Chris had intended. Fortunately, the driver was more than a little preoccupied at the time, and missed the absence of any subtlety.

'Ah – his mother is my sister, Grace,' replied Benford. 'She's in real estate – you know, property. Very successful. She married Bob just after my Stockton was born. Bob worked in New Jersey back then.'

'Doing what?' asked Chris.

'He's an architect.'

That didn't tell Chris anything useful (or interesting). He decided to probe a little deeper.

'Are you going to tell his parents about him going missing?'

Benford looked quite shocked at the idea. 'There's no need for that. I mean, I don't want to worry them.'

Chris pointed out that they needed to turn left at the next junction. Mr Carter started to signal right away, even though they were still almost a quarter of a mile from the turning.

'Do they have e-mail at home?' asked Chris.

'His father does,' Benford replied. 'And Jace too, but I don't think Grace would know how to work it.'

Now *that* was interesting. Chris digested the information carefully as Benford eased the car around the corner on to the Spirebrook road.

'Why do you ask?' Benford wanted to know.

'It's just that Jace hasn't called home while he's been with us. He's used the e-mail, though.'

Mr Carter actually looked surprised and concerned by that fact. 'He has? Who has he been speaking to?'

'I don't know. His dad, maybe?'

'I don't think so. His father is . . . away. On business.'

Chris tried hard to look straight ahead, as if all he cared about was idle chatter and directing the American to his front door. He couldn't help but notice, though, that Mr Carter looked very uncomfortable. Chris decided to change the subject and to approach Mr Carter from a sneaky direction.

'Does Jace have any brothers or sisters?'

'No. He's an only child.'

Chris nodded. 'Me too,' he said. Mr Carter smiled at him. 'And I've only got one parent too,' Chris continued.

Mr Carter stopped smiling. 'What do you mean by that?' he said, abruptly.

'My mum left home when I was tiny,' Chris explained, 'and you said Jace's father doesn't live at home.'

'Did I?'

'Yeah. You said his dad had e-mail and that Jace had e-mail too. Like they didn't live together.'

Mr Carter opened his mouth as if he was going to argue the point, but he stumbled over the words while they were still in his head.

'Yes, that's right. His father had . . . his father moved out to California in 1989. Jace still sees him; he visits with him quite often, in fact. He and Grace are still friends.'

'Oh.'

There was an awkward silence. Mr Carter looked increasingly uncomfortable and not just because of Chris's stunning investigative questioning. The traffic was quite thick through here and they got stuck behind a bus which was belching diesel smoke from its exhaust. Chris reassured him that they were quite close to home.

'Why did Jace's father move?'

Mr Carter shot Chris a look as if he was starting to get tired of questions he didn't want to answer.

'Uh – a variety of things. Work. These things just happen, you know?'

Chris nodded as if he understood and agreed. In fact, he had become convinced that there was more to this than met the eye. Something was nagging at him; some small detail that he'd overlooked.

'I guess Jace must really like aeroplanes, huh?' he asked. Chopping and changing the subject like this seemed to work really well with Mr Carter. Chris thought he could see beads of sweat on the American's brow.

'Not really.'

'But he flies a great deal . . .' Chris insisted.

'What is this?' demanded Benford. 'Why are you asking all these questions?'

'I'm sorry,' Chris replied, genuinely sorry to have offended Mr Carter (although he couldn't see how he had). He waited for a moment and then offered a sincere: 'I'm sure he'll be all right, you know.'

'I had hoped you were looking after him!' Mr Carter muttered.

'I'm sorry,' Chris said again.

'No, no, I'm the one that should be sorry. I didn't mean to jump down your throat.' Mr Carter rubbed his chin. 'I'm just a little edgy.'

'That's OK,' said Chris. They were almost at the end of his road. He pointed the turning out to Mr Carter and sat in silence as they finally emerged from behind the noxious shadow of the bus. Mr Carter drove the short distance along the tree-lined street to Chris's house. The car glided to a halt and Mr Carter applied the handbrake and switched off the engine.

'Actually,' he said in a more friendly fashion, looking much happier now that he didn't have to drive, 'Jace has hardly ever flown at all. He demanded a window seat when we came over here so he could watch it all happen.'

Chris nodded. The small bell that was alerting him to something being wrong about this situation was ringing even louder. If Jace's father lived on the west coast and his mother on the east, how could Jace visit his father 'often' without flying? Chris was sure he'd read somewhere that it took days to drive across the country, or to take the train.

He decided not to say anything. He'd got the impression

Mr Carter wasn't happy at how close Chris was getting to the truth – even though Chris felt further away than ever.

The American was looking past him at the front door. There was no-one in sight.

'Doesn't look like he's back yet,' Benford sighed.

'No,' agreed Chris. 'I promise I'll call Sean as soon as I hear from him.'

He opened the door and stepped out. It occurred to him as he set foot on the pavement that he'd been nervous about being stuck with Mr Carter. If he'd decided one thing in the last half-hour, it was that Benford Carter might not be telling the whole truth, but that he was about as likely to be a criminal as the lady who did the school crossing patrol.

He ducked down to look through the door.

'This will all turn out for the best,' he said, trying to be reassuring. Then he closed the car door and ran up the drive to his front porch. Turning the key in the lock, he went inside without looking back and made straight for the phone.

He punched out the seven digits from memory.

'Nicky? It's Chris. Get over here – I have to talk to you.'

Six

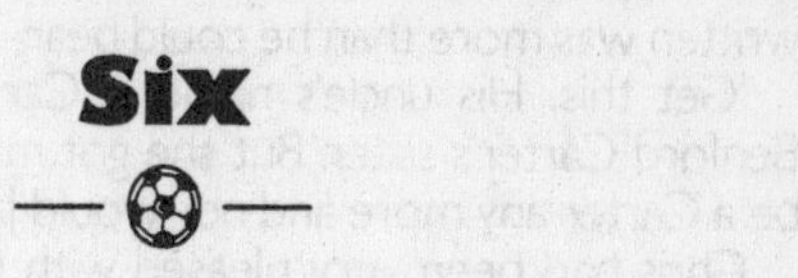

'Just read the e-mail!' Nicky insisted.

Chris drained the last of his Coke and took the glass to the sink. He rinsed it out quickly and stood it on the draining board, then went back for Nicky's glass, repeating the operation.

'Chris!' Nicky scolded him.

'I can't!' Chris insisted. 'Look, it might not be anything important. It could just be a message from a mate, or a girlfriend or something. I can't just read it!'

Nicky sorted through the biscuits at the bottom of the tin in front of him, looking dismayed at Chris's stubbornness.

'It seems to me that you're not really that interested in finding out who Jace really is, or what he's up to.' He looked up and pointed at Chris with a broken half of a digestive biscuit. 'Why didn't you tell the guy from the American embassy about the e-mail?'

'He'd gone by then,' insisted Chris.

'Well, let's give him a call now,' said Nicky.

Chris shook his head. 'I can't. He told me not to. He said he'd contact me.'

Nicky scowled. Chris had asked him round to talk about the great Jace mystery and all they had done so far was eat some biscuits (which were on the point of going stale) and drink Coke. Nicky liked his detective work to have a bit more excitement.

He also liked to fill A4 pads with strange notations which were supposed to provide him with flashes of insight. All the best TV policemen did it. So far, all Nicky had written was the word 'JACE', underlined three times.

'OK. If you're not going to read the e-mail, what have you found out that's so important?'

'Well, for one, his name isn't Jace Carter.'

Nicky looked up with a surprised expression on his face which quickly changed to dismay. He looked down at his pad, as if the prospect of having to cross out the only word he had written was more than he could bear.

'Get this. His uncle's name is Carter, right? His mum is Benford Carter's sister. But she got married, so she wouldn't be a Carter any more and nor would Jace.'

Chris had been very pleased with this piece of deductive reasoning once he'd puzzled it out. He wasn't happy that Nicky managed to look very unimpressed.

'If they're divorced, Jace's mother might have gone back to her maiden name. Your mum doesn't call herself Stephens any more, does she?'

That double painful reminder knocked Chris off-balance a bit, but he stuck to his guns, convinced that his first impressions were right. 'It's not quite the same thing. Jace still gets on with his dad; sees him a lot. Would he have changed his name back to Carter? I don't think so. I think his real name is Goodman. And that's another thing. Jace's dad lives in California; Benford lives in Newark; Jace is supposed to go to Mount Graham school in Newark. But when Jace goes to visit his father, he doesn't fly, he goes by car.'

The significance of this was lost on Nicky, who had only a sketchy knowledge of the geography of his home town, never mind a distant continent that didn't have a single team in the Premier League.

Chris sighed. 'It's 2,500 miles across America, Nicky. I looked it up. Two days solid driving, without a break. No-one does that any more.'

Nicky didn't look as if he thought this was very conclusive either. He hadn't added any notes to his pad. In fact, at this point he even put his pen down.

'Is that it?'

'It means Jace can't actually live in Newark,' Chris insisted. By the time he finished the sentence he wasn't so sure himself any more. 'At least that's what I think it means. It would make some kind of sense out of why the other guys from Mount Graham all hate him – he doesn't even go to their school. They probably think he's only made the trip because of his uncle being in charge.'

'Which is what you thought a couple of days ago,' sighed Nicky, folding his arms defiantly. Short of putting the A4 pad away, this was about as close as he could get to saying that Chris was wasting their time.

Chris started to wonder if maybe Nicky wasn't right. After all, what did he care if Jace was in trouble with the law in the USA? The guy had gone out of his way to keep his distance and he was clearly lying about something, whether it was serious or not.

The trouble was, he was starting to like Jace, though he had no idea why.

'OK, maybe you're right,' Chris sighed.

'We forget about Jace Carter?' said Nicky.

'No,' said Chris. 'We read the e-mail.'

Nicky almost beat him upstairs. He waited impatiently while Chris restarted the computer and found the duplicate of the file he had hidden away.

Chris hesitated, and then opened it up.

The sender's address was LMarion@AOL.com. That meant they couldn't tell where the sender lived, but it was a reasonable guess that it was in the USA, where America On-Line was strongest. The time it was sent also suggested the same thing – it would have been during the night in the UK, but in the afternoon in the USA – especially if the sender was in California. L. Marion was likely to be the person's name – it didn't look like a company label.

That was as much as they could tell from the header.

The message itself didn't reveal much more. It read:

> JACE
>
> YOUR FATHER WANTS YOU TO SIT TIGHT AND BE SENSIBLE. SOMEONE WILL MAKE CONTACT WITH YOU. DON'T DO ANYTHING FOOLISH. BY THE WAY, YOUR MUM SAYS HI AS WELL.

There was no sign-off at the bottom.

'What do you make of that?' asked Nicky.

Chris was re-reading the message, hoping it would become clearer. 'Your father wants you to sit tight,' he recited. He was trying to break the message down into pieces, to see if it could be understood that way.

'That's clear enough,' said Nicky. 'He's supposed to stay here. Look here – later on – where it says he's to be sensible. I guess his dad wants him somewhere he can find him.'

'I don't think so,' said Chris. 'It's not from his father, is it? "Your father wants you to sit tight." '

'Maybe someone who works for his dad sent it . . . what difference does it make? It's still clear that his dad wants him to hang on here until someone gets in touch . . . do you think that means the bloke from the embassy?'

Chris shrugged. 'I suppose.' He continued to scan the message, looking for any hidden clues that would help him decide what to do next.

'The thing is . . .' he said to Nicky a moment later, 'as soon as he read this message, Jace did a runner. He didn't want to see Ripley. If he thought his dad had sent Ripley, wouldn't he have been glad to see him?'

'Maybe he's frightened of his dad . . .' Nicky started to say, but then stopped. From what little they knew of Jace, he got on brilliantly with his dad.

'Perhaps we'd do better trying to find Jace than sitting around here going mad trying to work it all out,' sighed Nicky. 'It's not down to us to decide whether Jace is involved in anything shady or not. We should just track him down and hand him over to this Ripley bloke.'

Chris nodded, agreeing that this was *possibly* the right thing to do. However, there was the obvious practical difficulty to deal with first.

'Where do you suggest we look?' asked Chris.

That was the final frustration as far as Nicky was concerned. He made a frustrated noise in his throat and turned away from the screen to throw himself face down on Chris's bed.

'I'm getting really fed up with this,' he said.

Chris read the message one last time, then closed the file and switched off the computer. 'I know what you mean – I don't know what to do either. I mean, supposing Jace turns up; should we *really* just wait for Ripley to come and get him? I mean, what if Ripley isn't who he says he is?'

'I thought you looked at his ID . . .' said Nicky, looking even less happy now that Chris had found another way to complicate the story.

'Yeah, but how do I know what a real US government ID looks like?' Chris only had one basis for comparison; the ID Ripley had shown him looked similar to the ones he saw each week when the titles rolled up for *The X-Files*. The fact was, all he had seen was Ripley's photo, some printed letters that said 'US GOVERNMENT' and a few squiggles that might have been signatures. His dad had something similar that he wore at work.

Nicky sat up. 'Well, we can soon sort that out,' he said, with new conviction.

'How?'

'Call the embassy in London. That's where he said he worked, right?'

'Yes, but he said *not* to call.'

Nicky rolled his eyes back and clenched his teeth. Chris realised that Nicky wasn't going to be put off by such an instruction.

'Look, we just ask for his extension. If he answers, we hang up. If not, then we know he's a fake!'

Chris thought about this plan for a moment. It did seem like a fair solution to their difficulties. If Ripley really was who he said he was, then they could just leave everything to him. On the other hand, if he was a fake, then maybe Jace was in more trouble than they had ever feared.

They went downstairs and called directory enquiries.

Armed with the number of the embassy, Chris dialled and held the receiver so that Nicky could hear the conversation as well. A woman with a strong accent answered the phone and announced that they had called the US embassy.

'Good morning,' said Chris. 'I'd like to speak to Mr Ripley, please.'

'Which department is he in?' the woman asked.

The boys looked at each other in some despair, foiled at the first fence.

'Uh – I'm not actually sure,' Chris confessed.

'Well, would he be trade, or diplomatic, or legal . . .?' the woman suggested. Chris cut her off at that third option.

'It could be legal!' he blurted out, clutching at the offered straw. A moment later, his confidence waning, he added: 'I think.'

The woman was actually quite sympathetic. 'I'll look in the directory,' she said warmly. 'I'm sure I'll track him down for you. Just hold a moment, would you?'

They waited patiently, the line humming a country and western ballad while they held on. There were a couple of clicks and what sounded like a distant, echoing voice. Abruptly, the woman came back on the line again.

'Did you say Ripley?' she asked.

'That's right.'

'I can't find a Ripley,' she said in a distant sort of way. Chris could imagine her scanning through the directory again to make sure. 'Are you sure he's on the staff here?'

'That's what he said,' Chris replied, and then a thought popped into his head from nowhere. 'Hang on – he might be new. He said he was from California and hadn't got used to our climate yet.'

'Ah!' the woman said. 'Just hold for a moment longer, would you?'

More country and western. Nicky wrinkled his nose in disgust. 'What kind of music do you suppose they play on British embassy phones?' he asked. 'Oasis? Phil Collins?'

'More likely 'Land Of Hope And Glory' or something,' muttered Chris, who shared Nicky's dislike of country. 'I expect they play this stuff to put people off who want to emigrate to America.' He grinned.

'It's so *depressing*!' agreed Nicky. He stepped back, put on a miserable face and made a whining noise through his nose that was supposed to sound like a pedal steel guitar. 'My dog died while I was in prison!' he sang, with the worst American accent Chris had ever heard.

The woman returned to the line. Chris gestured to Nicky to shut up. They were both still giggling.

'Are you sure about the name?' she asked.

'Yes ma'am,' said Chris, mimicking her accent without realising he was doing it. Nicky covered his mouth with his hand and spluttered helplessly.

The woman suddenly sounded a lot less friendly. 'You

wouldn't be playing some kind of practical joke here, would you, young man?'

'No!' insisted Chris.

She didn't sound convinced. 'Well, whoever your Mr *Ripley* is,' she said, emphasising the name with some contempt, 'when you next see him, tell him it's a criminal offence to falsely identify yourself as an employee of the government of the United States.'

'He had ID!' Chris told her quickly.

'Whatever he had and whoever he works for, he is not connected with the American embassy. If you see this man again, I suggest you contact your British police immediately.'

'Uh – I will . . .' Chris stumbled.

'Thank you for calling,' the woman said. 'Have a nice day.'

The line clicked as it went dead.

'Cool,' said Nicky. 'I wasn't sure if she'd actually say that.' He made an attempt to copy her. 'Have a nice day!'

'Give up, Nicky. Didn't you hear what she said? Ripley's a fake!'

'Oh, I bet it's just a mistake –' Nicky began. Chris put the phone down, shaking his head.

'I don't think so. My guess is –' He stopped, realising that Nicky was looking past him, down the hall towards the front door. Chris turned.

Now what? he thought. More strangers, walking up the drive towards the front door. Two older men – about the same age as his father. One was reed-slim, and tall, with a worried expression highlighted by dark rings under his eyes and lines around his mouth and forehead. His complexion was quite dark and his hair thinning. He looked dishevelled, as if he had been sleeping in the casual clothes he wore.

The other man, walking just behind the first, was dressed more smartly and looked much more at ease. A half-smile played around his lips. He was shorter than his companion, but a little stockier. He had intelligent, deep-set eyes. As well as a sharp grey suit and black shoes that shone brilliantly, he was wearing a hat.

They were an odd-matched pair, Chris thought, as they reached the door. As he watched them approach, Chris stopped to consider that they might be salesmen, or Jehovah's witnesses. He couldn't think of anything, though, that fitted the way they looked so different, and that made him decide, long before he pulled the door back on its chain, that it wouldn't be a surprise at all if they were something to do with Jace.

It turned out that was a good call.

'Hi. Excuse me . . . I'm looking for Jace Goodman,' said the scruffy man. 'I'm his father.'

Nicky wasn't impressed with the idea of being sent to the kitchen to make tea, but it did ensure that the drink was made in record time. Chris took the two men through to the living room, where the three of them sat in almost complete silence. The smartly dressed man looked around the room and complimented Chris on having a nice home, as if they had come for dinner or something. Other than that, nothing was said until Nicky arrived with mugs of steaming tea, a half-filled milk bottle and the sugar bowl. He had to go back for the spoons.

So much for trying to impress anyone.

Chris used the time to try and collect his thoughts. There was no doubt in his mind that the scruffy man was Jace's father. Robert Goodman had shown Chris his passport at the door and a picture of Jace when he was younger. However, you only had to look at Mr Goodman to know that he and Jace were related. They had the same eyes, the same tight-lipped mouth. Jace's hair was a little darker (and there was more of it), but it had the same tendency to curl up around the ends.

Sitting in silence waiting for an explanation reminded Chris of being with Jace too.

Mr Goodman apologised for looking and sounding a bit rough. He had literally stepped off the plane at Heathrow just a few hours before and had come right here. He hadn't had a lot of sleep over the last few days. Chris noticed that he hadn't shaved for at least that long. He looked a mess.

His companion, who was introduced as Mr Jackson, didn't intrude on this part of the conversation at all. He sat there, smiling politely, thanking Nicky for the tea and asking for some more milk. Then he put the mug down beside the chair he was sitting on and never touched it again.

Finally, Mr Goodman got to the point.

'Is my son here, Chris?'

Chris shook his head, still sizing the situation up, reluctant to speak. He wanted to make absolutely sure before –

'We're not sure where he is,' said Nicky, jumping in. 'This guy called, see, and . . .'

'What Nicky is trying to say,' Chris broke in, 'is that Jace went off with one of the other guys in the American team. He'll be back later.'

Nicky's expression showed that he was shocked to have been squashed like that by Chris. To Chris's relief, he didn't say anything, although his expression seemed an enormous giveaway from where Chris was sitting.

If he noticed, Mr Goodman didn't say anything.

'No practice today?' he asked.

'Not today,' Chris replied.

Everyone sat quietly for a minute. Chris deliberately avoided looking at Nicky, who he was sure would still be wearing his 'What the hell is going on?' face.

'What time do you expect him back?' asked Mr Goodman.

'I'm not sure,' said Chris, and he stopped there to clear his throat. 'He might be out all day.'

Mr Goodman looked at the other man, his face lined with concern. There was no clue in Mr Jackson's expression at all.

'I need to see Jace quite urgently.'

'I'm sorry, Mr Goodman, but I can't get in touch with him until later. I'll leave him a message in case he comes back while we're out . . .'

Jace's father looked at the other man again, then fixed his eyes on Chris before speaking. 'I don't think you can reach us, either. Perhaps we'll just call back later.'

He stood up, then froze in place when he realised that Mr Jackson still hadn't moved. After hesitating for a moment, he sat down again, reaching for his tea. He took a long gulp, almost scalding himself on the drink, then put the mug down rapidly.

'Sorry . . .' he coughed.

Mr Jackson still hadn't moved, nor removed his gaze from

the faces of the two boys. Chris tried to avoid staring into those dark eyes, but twice he was trapped and it felt almost as if Jackson could see into his head. Fortunately – or not, depending on your point of view – he spent even more time scrutinising Nicky, who was starting to look very uncomfortable, perched on the arm of the sofa where Chris was seated.

Mr Goodman had recovered from his mild choking fit. 'Is – uh! – Jace getting on OK, with the other guys, I mean?'

'Sure,' said Chris, enthusiastically. A way to turn the question to his advantage suddenly occurred to him. 'Those Mount Graham guys stick together like glue, don't they?' There was a long delay before Mr Goodman nodded in reply. 'Has he been playing soccer for long?' Chris asked, determined not to let up. For the first time, he saw Jackson twitch.

'No . . .' said Jace's father in a low voice. 'Not long.'

'He's pretty good. Are you staying for the games next weekend?'

'I don't think so.'

'That's a pity. It'll be a lot of fun. I know Jace would love it if you could see him play. Still, there are plenty of opportunities before then.'

Mr Goodman looked up, seeming quite confused.

'Practice games,' explained Chris. 'I bet you're looking forward to seeing him play.'

Goodman's face didn't look very thrilled as he muttered something in reply.

Jackson was now watching Chris even more closely. Chris hid behind his tea, taking a sip. Mr Goodman picked his mug up again too and turned it round in his hands before drinking a little more.

'Jace tells me he likes riding,' said Chris.

Mr Goodman looked up and nodded. 'There's a ranch near where I live in California. Jace comes riding with me when he visits –'

'Ah!' exclaimed Chris, as if all he had been doing was making conversation. After a while, he made a point of looking at his watch.

'Look,' he said, 'I'm sorry to be rude, but Nicky and I have to go out.' He rose to his feet and gave Nicky his mug

(Fiorentini looked even more confused than ever). He collected the milk bottle and the sugar bowl, and stepped towards the door. Mr Goodman took the hint, finished his tea and stood up. Jackson remained still, watching the show with his glittering eyes mostly fixed on Chris.

Chris pushed Nicky towards the kitchen carrying the various bits of crockery.

'Where will you be staying?' he asked Mr Goodman.

Jace's father looked as if he couldn't have told Chris what day it was, never mind know anything like that. He flicked his eyes back at Jackson, who was now right behind him.

'I'm not sure,' he said awkwardly. 'That is, I don't think you can get in touch with us . . . until we've found somewhere, I mean.' He obviously realised he was almost talking nonsense and closed his mouth.

'OK,' Chris replied lightly.

'We'll call back later, if that's OK.'

'O – no problem,' Chris said, smiling, managing to avoid using the word OK yet again. He stepped through the door.

He wasn't sure if he heard something whispered between the two men or not – and he certainly couldn't make it out – but there was a very short delay before Mr Goodman got to the hall and a slightly longer one before Jackson followed.

'We'll see you later on, then,' Goodman said.

'OK,' said Chris (so much for trying to be different). He opened the door.

Goodman stepped through, pausing on the step. Chris looked back to find Jackson still standing in the hall, showing no immediate sign of going anywhere. His eyes were boring into Chris's skull. Luckily, he was distracted when Nicky dropped a mug in the kitchen, and Chris was able to look away. For a moment there, he'd wondered if he was being hypnotised.

He stepped past Jackson towards the kitchen and caught Nicky picking up broken shards of crockery.

When he looked back, Jackson had turned and was doffing his hat slightly like an old-fashioned gentleman. Chris noticed that his hair was silver-grey.

'Bye!' he said quickly.

Jackson walked to the front door and Chris followed to

close it. Now that he was behind Jackson, he noticed the man had his hair in a pony-tail at the back.

Once both the men were across the doorstep, Chris felt a little more at ease. Jackson walked straight past Mr Goodman, stepping down the slope of the drive, eyes straight ahead. Chris noticed the front of a car parked out on the street. It looked like some kind of sports car – a low, blood-red machine with flip-up headlights.

'Mr Goodman,' he called, as quietly as he could. Jace's father looked round. 'Is Jace in some kind of trouble?'

'Now, why would you think that?' came the reply, only it wasn't from Mr Goodman, it was from Jackson, who had spun round in the drive.

Chris felt his courage slipping away. He didn't like Jackson at all. There was something quite spooky about the man. He was too smooth, too self-assured. He didn't *feel* right.

'There was this other man . . .' Chris began.

Jackson was grinning, taking a step back up the drive.

'And?'

'And he said he was from the government – your government, the US government,' Chris stumbled, suddenly aware that whereas Mr Goodman had a very obvious American accent, Jackson did not. He sounded as if he came from – actually, the more he thought about it, Chris realised that he couldn't place the way Jackson spoke at all. It was as if his voice was a smooth automated version, with any slightly unusual tones stripped out, leaving just the words on their own.

'Really?' said Jackson, and Chris thought he was mocking him.

'That's what he said. He wanted to find Jace too and said he'd come back later. He told me Jace was in trouble.' Chris made a point of not mentioning that Ripley had also told him that Jace's father had been arrested. Somehow, Chris didn't find himself believing that Jackson was some kind of policeman . . .

'It isn't anything you need to concern yourself about, young man,' Jackson replied tartly. 'Just let Jace know that his father is looking for him. Ask him who he would prefer to deal with; his own father, or some spook working for the American government. He should sit tight, wait for us to come back and not do anything foolish.' He stared at Chris, as if making sure that Chris had got the message. Chris was pretty sure he had.

'Anything else?' he asked.

'Yeah,' said Mr Goodman, his voice sounding a little dry and cracked. 'Tell him his mother would want him to do the right thing too.'

With that, Jace's father turned from the door and made his way to the car. Looking at Jackson, Chris thought he saw a hint of annoyance in the man's face before he too stepped from the drive. A moment later, a powerful engine fired up, and the sports car cruised away from the kerb. Chris listened as it slowed to make a turn, then it revved up and roared off into the distance.

Nicky was now at the front door with him.

'What was that all about?' he asked, as the sound of the car finally vanished under the hum of traffic from the main road.

'You heard what that Jackson guy said; it's none of our business,' replied Chris. 'All we have to do is give Jace a message.'

Nicky was clearly amazed at Chris's quiet determination not to get involved. Normally, Chris hated it when people told him what to do.

'So, is that all we're going to do?' he asked, and then Chris grinned, and there was a mischievous, stubborn glint in his eye.

'Well, we can't deliver the message unless we find Jace first, can we?' he replied.

Seven

Oldcester was not a huge city. From Spirebrook, where Chris and Nicky lived, it was a twenty-minute bus journey to the city centre. Oldcester's heart was built around two parallel streets that ran for about half a mile in an almost dead straight line. Between the two streets there was the main shopping district, known as Fair Market, the town hall with its tree-ringed square, and a small museum. At one end, the two streets crossed the river using Victorian iron bridges painted in the city colours; one of them ran past Star Park, the home of Oldcester United, the other swung off to the south towards Memorial Park. At its other end, beyond Fair Market, that same road detoured around the railway station, while its partner bent up and away towards Spirebrook and the western side of the city.

Shops, galleries, a theatre, two cinemas, banks, more building societies than you could count, an underground car park and bus garage, a hideous fountain and a huge roofless cafe called The Wanderers all nestled in that small space. It was always crowded – especially on Saturdays, when there was a small market in the square in front of the town hall. To the north, there were office buildings, all glass and polished metal, reflecting light back down on to the city centre, which glowed day and night with neon signs and bright shop lights. The old buildings had been scrubbed clean and glowed in shades of pink and white like freshly bathed children. Excluding what took place on alternate Saturdays at Star Park (plus mid-week fixtures, of course), everything that was ever going to happen in Oldcester happened in Fair Market.

Chris and Nicky got off the bus on St James's Street and strolled through the pedestrianised area to The Wanderers.

This had once been roofed over in glass, but during World War Two, the Germans had dropped the one bomb they ever landed on Oldcester right in the middle of The Wanderers. The glass had never been replaced; only the iron beams remained.

It was a wide circle where six small streets met. Now there were no cars, the centre was wholly given over to a vast number of blue and red tables and chairs set around the fountain. Every shop front that opened on to the circle (and several down the side streets) had been converted into a food bar, featuring cuisine from around the world – Indian, Chinese, French, Mexican, Italian (and not just Pizzaland!), Thai. You could have breakfast, brunch, dinner, tea, supper and late-night snacks, and you could do it every day for a fortnight without visiting a single bar twice. There was a shop selling Belgian chocolate; there was a bar selling 111 varieties of ice-cream. There were sandwich bars, crêperies, coffee shops and a vegetarian 'emporium' (which never seemed to be that busy, but then it was 'sandwiched' between McDonalds and Kentucky Fried Chicken).

Finally, there were two pubs. One of them served food that was renowned as being the worst in Oldcester. The Market Bell sold steak and kidney pie, a huge slab of meat and pastry, with three veg and a lake of gravy for £3.50.

They found Sean Priest and Stefan Brodenberg sitting at one of the closest tables to the pub. Sean had a packet of crisps; Stefan was about £1.75's-worth into his steak and kidney pie.

'Over here!' called Priest, as soon as he saw them.

They picked their way between the tables. There was a short pause while they found some chairs before they could sit with the Oldcester coach and his Danish guest. Stefan looked delighted to see them and paused in his demolition of lunch as they sat down.

'You guys want anything?' asked Priest.

'A burger from Mad Jack's would be great!' said Nicky instantly. Chris agreed to have the same, to avoid making Priest queue twice at different stalls. He picked up his mobile phone from the table and went off, disappearing into the crowd.

'You guys are mad,' commented Stefan, pointing at his food with his knife. 'You should have a proper meal, like this.'

Nicky shrank back as if he had been told to eat earthworms. 'Kidney? Yeccchhh.'

Stefan poked his fork into a particularly large chunk of the aforementioned meat and slipped it into his mouth. His expression became quite overjoyed as he chewed.

'Good food!' he insisted. 'Look at all this – and what burger will you get for £3.50? A skinny little thing, with some skinny little fries. At least in America there would be a big piece of meat in the burger, but over here it's not enough to feed a mouse.'

Chris could tell that Nicky wasn't buying that argument. Whenever he got hungry, he just went home and let his mother whip up one of her enormous meals. Eating one of Mad Jack's burgers was just one of the things you did in Fair Market – it had nothing to do with food.

Stefan finished chewing what was in his mouth, then sat back in his chair, drinking from a cold bottle of Coke, with the warm sun on his face. Then his eyes flittered open.

'So, you've found our lost sheep, then?'

'Yes,' said Chris. 'It's all my fault – I forgot Jace said he was coming into town to go shopping for some souvenirs.'

Stefan frowned a little. 'It's very naughty of him. He was supposed to be at practice this morning.'

Chris fidgeted with the cuff of his jacket. 'You can't expect him to keep pretending about the football all the time, Stefan,' he said.

The Dane's pale eyes widened very slightly. 'Ah, you know about that?' he asked.

'Not much of a secret, really,' scoffed Nicky. 'He can't play at all! How did you expect him to pass as one of the team?'

Stefan spread his hands wide in a resigned gesture. 'It was just for practice; just for show. He wasn't going to play in any matches.'

'Even so –'

Stefan cut him short. 'It was the only thing that could be done. Mr Carter said Jace had to come with us, because he was in trouble. Stockton wasn't very happy about staying behind, but it meant Jace could travel on Mr Carter's passport, pretending to be his son.'

'They look alike, do they, Stockton and Jace?'

'Close enough. You know what passport pictures look like! I think a creature from Mars could use my passport and no-one would know! Provided he was good-looking, anyway.'

The boys laughed. Stefan swept another pile of food on to his fork and shovelled it into his mouth. Chris gave him a moment.

'So he just used Stockton's ticket? Pretended he was Stockton Carter?'

Stefan nodded, pointing to his mouth to show he wasn't ready to speak just yet.

'What did you tell the other members of the team?'

'The same as we told you. We left it until the last minute, when we were on the plane, then we told them that Stockton was sick and that Jace would take his place. We said he had to pretend to be part of the team, or your people might not let him play. Benford said he thought Jace was a good enough athlete to carry it off.'

Nicky made the snorting sound he always made when he heard something he could scarcely believe. 'But he's completely useless!' He smirked. Chris had to remind himself that Nicky hadn't actually seen Jace play.

'True . . .' said Stefan, before he took another mouthful.

Chris nodded, mentally ticking off another piece of the puzzle. 'But when you got here, he didn't pretend to be Stockton Carter, he was Jace Carter.'

They had to wait for Stefan to finish before they got the answer.

'A necessary compromise.' The Dane held up his hands and gestured with the right. 'He couldn't be Stockton Carter; he might make mistakes; not answer when he was called. The other boys too.' He switched his attention to his left hand. 'And he couldn't be Jace Goodman either. That was the whole point, of course. We had to make Jace Goodman disappear, you see? So . . .' He pressed both hands together. 'Jace Carter.' Stefan threw both his hands up into the air, then used them to pick up his knife and fork once more. 'It wasn't my plan,' he said.

'So how much do you know about what's going on?' asked Chris quickly, before the Dane could fill his mouth again. 'Just why did Jace have to get out of America in such a hurry?'

'Who knows?' Stefan shrugged.

Chris couldn't accept that. 'But Benford must have said something! Or else why did you go along with it?'

'Ah, he's the boss,' Stefan replied with a sideways nod of his head. 'And he made it sound very important. I don't care; I'd rather play football.' It looked as if he might leave it there and continue eating, but he paused with the next forkful only partway to his mouth. 'Look, it was enough for me that Benford was worried. But, if you want to know the truth, the way I hear it, the boy's father was in big trouble with the law and Jace was in danger, OK?'

'In danger?' cried Nicky, who was more interested now that there was a bit of drama. 'What – from his father?'

Stefan, eating again now, rocked his head from side to side in a maybe, maybe not gesture. Nicky flashed a look at Chris.

'Mightn't his dad come looking for him?' asked Chris.

'Maybe,' mumbled Stefan. He wiped a piece of carrot from the corner of his mouth. 'The important thing is that he sticks with us, right? All he's done so far is get Benford worried. You tell him, as long as he is with his friends, nothing can happen to him.'

'Right,' said Chris.

Stefan nodded and mopped up the last of his dinner. By the time he had finished it, Priest was on his way back carrying a tray from Mad Jack's. He placed his mobile phone on the table and handed over the food.

'So,' he asked, 'where is our runaway?'

'In town somewhere,' said Chris, looking around. 'He called an hour ago, asking us to meet him.' Priest poured some brown sugar into the coffee he had bought himself, and stirred it in.

'Great. You can tell him from me that he'd better have a good reason for scaring us all like that.'

Stefan looked a little uneasy. 'Aren't we waiting until he gets here?'

'What for?' replied Priest. 'Chris and Nicky can bring him to the bowling when he shows up. Or there's the disco tonight, if he's much later than about three o'clock. We've got twenty other kids to take care of – we can't expect Iain and Benford to do all the work!'

'I suppose not . . .' replied Stefan softly.

'We'll call Benford to let him know the good news,' Priest told Chris. 'Make sure that once Jace turns up, you keep a tight hold on him, OK?'

'You can count on it,' replied Chris.

'Good.' Priest drank his coffee quickly, washing down the crisps. 'Come on, Stefan. Time we were gone.'

The Dane stood up slowly, looking around as Priest took his jacket from the back of the chair and picked up his mobile.

'See you guys later,' Priest said, and the two men set off through the crowds. Chris watched them go.

Nicky was already halfway into his burger. It oozed ketchup and mustard as he took another large bite.

'Brilliant . . .' he mumbled (clearly better adapted to eating and speaking than Stefan). Chris had to wait to see if he meant the burger or the outcome of their conversation. Nicky chewed slowly and he still had half the last mouthful between his teeth when he started to recap. 'So, that's Stefan, Sean and Benford on the one hand, who want us to find Jace,' he said, counting on his fingers. 'There's this Ripley guy, who wants to find Jace; and then there's Jace's dad and that other bloke –'

'Jackson.'

'– him, who wants us to find Jace.'

That seemed a fair summing up of the basics. Nicky frowned heavily, as if he had been hoping this meeting with Priest and Stefan was going to help clear things up. Chris knew just how much it had done the opposite.

'Have you also noticed,' said Chris, 'that each of them tells us that it's best if they find Jace first? That it wouldn't be such a good idea if anyone else beat them to him?'

'So who's right?'

'How should I know?' laughed Chris. 'Do we trust his dad, who may or may not be a crook; Ripley, who may or may not be a government agent; or do we trust Sean, which means trusting Benford Carter, who's told so many lies he's bound to be caught up in this whole thing somehow.'

Nicky looked thoroughly miserable. 'Why did you tell them we knew where Jace was? If there is anything suss about Benford Carter, now he'll be watching out for us.'

'Exactly. He can't watch us and look out for Jace. If we hear from Mr Goodman again, I'm going to tell him the same thing. With luck, that means they'll all be watching us and not searching for Jace.'

'And this is a good thing?' moaned Nicky, putting down the last half of his burger.

'That depends,' said Chris, 'on whether we ever find him.'

⚽

'What did Benford say?' Sean asked, as he took back his phone.

'He's very relieved. The sooner Jace meets up with Chris and Nicky, the better.' Stefan looked down at the pavement as they hurried towards the stairs that led down to the car park.

'You OK?' asked Priest.

'Sure,' said Stefan. 'I just want this to be over.'

'I know,' agreed Priest. 'All this cloak and dagger stuff, it's like something out of a spy novel. Still, don't worry. You can rely on Chris to get Jace to see sense. He'll turn up soon enough.'

'I'm counting on it,' said Stefan.

⚽

Every time the sun went behind a cloud, Ripley shivered. He pulled his raincoat tighter and stepped back deeper into the doorway, sheltering from a wind that was more imaginary than real.

He kept his eyes on the boys at all times, watching as the one with the ruffled black hair ate his burger and then polished off the remains of his pal's. The black-haired kid looked quite miserable. It looked as if he was asking the other kid a lot of questions and not liking the answers.

Finally, they got up and made their way across The Wanderers, still talking animatedly. Ripley couldn't make out a word they were saying over the sound of the fountain and the general buzz of conversation from the scores of tables all around him. He barely heard it when his mobile phone started to warble.

He opened the phone and listened carefully. He didn't answer and he didn't break step as he threaded his way between the shoppers' bags and the few empty chairs. In the last moment before he closed the phone, he grinned and said, 'They'll lead me right to him.'

He put the phone back in his pocket, his eyes still fixed on where Chris and Nicky were walking towards one of the streets that radiated out from the circle. Staying well back and using the crowd as a shield, Ripley followed them out.

Jackson pressed the 'Call End' button on his mobile. Slipping it back into his jacket pocket, he rested both hands on the steering wheel.

'Contact has been made with your son,' he said, looking out through the sports car's windshield.

'Is he all right?' asked Mr Goodman from the passenger seat. His tired, bloodshot eyes were wide with stress.

'Don't worry yourself,' Jackson purred, and he leaned forward to start up the engine. 'Your family will soon be reunited. My people are very efficient.'

'And what happens then?' Goodman asked, his voice sounding raw with exhaustion and anxiety.

'You all disappear,' the other replied.

Eight

The lights in the main school building were growing brighter as the last of the spring daylight ebbed away. The dull bass throb of a dance track could be heard over the playground from as far away as the main gates. When the main doors opened, the music grew a little louder.

Chris stepped out into the evening air and made his way over to where another slender form was propped against the wall, sheltering from a slight evening breeze, and looking pretty miserable about it.

'My shift,' he said.

'About time,' moaned Jazz. This was clearly not his idea of a good time.

'It's only been fifteen minutes,' Chris rebuked him. Jazz made as if he was heading for the doors. 'Any sign of trouble?'

'No.'

'Any word from our guard dog?' Chris said, grinning, trying to get Jazz to lighten up.

'Get real!' Jazz snapped. 'Nothing's happened! All right? Can I go inside now?'

'Sure.' Chris shrugged, stepping aside.

Jazz swept passed and Chris heard the music swell and fade as his team mate passed through the doors. Chris moved round a little further and put himself more into the shadows. He thrust his hands into his pockets and waited.

He hoped his instincts were right. He couldn't think of a better time and place for Jace to make a reappearance. The American knew where the school was and he knew about the disco. It would be dark and there were plenty of places to hide – around the three main buildings, the gym, out on the sports field . . .

The minutes passed slowly, giving Chris plenty of time to wonder if he was right. He kept asking himself where Jace was going to go in a strange country, with no money, no friends – not even his jacket! He couldn't just run along to the embassy (assuming he could manage to get down to London) and ask for help – they were looking for him too. So, the only place he was going to find any help was from Chris, and that meant Chris had had to find somewhere neutral, somewhere dark, somewhere where all the various people looking for him wouldn't know the ground.

That meant here, tonight.

Chris pushed himself away from the wall restlessly. He wasn't having a good time. He had lied to his father about where Jace was; he'd lied to Sean Priest too. He seemed to have told quite a few lies in the last couple of years.

'It must be the company I keep,' he muttered to himself.

As if summoned by Chris thinking about him, Sean Priest chose that moment to emerge through the doors. He paused just outside and looked around. Chris knew he was looking for him. He had no reason at all to mistrust Priest, but there was no way he wanted to talk to him now. He remained in the shadows, watching. After a few moments, Priest went back inside.

Chris decided to put a little more distance between himself and the door, and moved towards the corner of the building. Three large, wheeled metal bins – each taller than Chris – stood in a small paved enclosure. They smelled a bit, which meant it wasn't likely that anyone would hang around them by choice. Chris walked over towards them.

It was even darker over on this side of the school, with no street lights or bright windows to throw illumination on the dark square of grass and the narrow pathways that ran close to the building. Chris was sheltered somewhat by the way the path dipped slightly, running between two small mounds capped by trees. That was how he saw the shadow before the shadow saw him.

In fact, he heard something before he saw it. A hiss, like a whisper, then running feet, thumping softly over grass. Chris froze on the spot. That was when he saw the shadow, moving quickly across in front of him from somewhere near the school gates towards the enclosure where the rubbish bins were kept. It was too dark to make out any details, but it looked about the right size for Jace. Or anyone else their age, for that matter.

Chris ducked down and took a few quick strides to the end of the wall. He thought he heard whispering again, but it stopped instantly. If it was Jace, it wasn't likely that he'd be speaking to anyone. On the other hand, it didn't sound like an adult's voice (if it was a voice).

That left one option. Chris took a deep breath and issued the challenge.

'Woof, woof!'

Nothing. A silence so deep it was like a weight. Concentrating harder, he could just make out the steady hum of traffic on the main road, but nothing closer, nothing more distinct.

He raised his voice just a notch. 'Woof, woof!'

He waited for the reply. Whoever it was must have heard him! If it was their 'watchdog', he'd have given the password by now. Chris could feel a small knot of anxiety in his stomach.

'Is that you, Jace?' he whispered, stalking a little closer. A dark shape loomed up in front of him, much closer than he had expected, and so fast he didn't have time to react. Hands reached out and grabbed him by the front of his jacket.

'What do we have here?' sneered a voice.

⚽

Russell found himself grinning, tucked away in his hiding place near the boiler room. It was the one place on the whole site from where he had a clear view of the school's front gates, the back entrance on to the new road and the entrance into the hall.

The small enclosure was where empty butane cylinders were kept prior to them being picked up by van every week. It was empty now, but still locked (Spirebrook Comprehensive took its security very seriously). That hadn't caused Russell any problem. He had climbed the fence, balancing on one of the posts to avoid the barbed wire, and had dropped inside. There were pipes and ducts near the wall and he was able to climb up about five metres to give himself a better view, keeping well out of sight.

The pipes were even warm.

Compared to some of the stunts he'd pulled a year or so ago, there was nothing very difficult about this one. He could recall some really high climbs, or the time he had wriggled through about a mile of air conditioning pipes to get into a sports warehouse.

Russell had a history. He wasn't proud of it, but it wasn't something he tried to pretend had never happened. His elder brother had forced him to take part in robberies from shops and warehouses around the city and they had become pretty good at it. Mick, though, was always trying to go that bit further. One day, he went too far and left Russ behind.

All that was left of those old days were the old skills. It felt funny hiding out like this when his motive wasn't thieving. It felt good.

Russell shook himself, bringing his mind back to the job at hand. He needed to concentrate, not lie around daydreaming. Maybe he was getting out of shape for this stuff . . .

Then he heard someone call, gently.

'Woof, woof!'

Russell grinned and lifted himself up from his hiding place. The code words had been Nicky's idea.

'Bow, wow!' he replied, feeling stupid. 'That you, Chris?'

No answer. He scanned the immediate area around the enclosure, looking for the source of the voice. He couldn't see anything. Cautiously, noiselessly, he dropped to the floor, then climbed up the fence and over on to the roadway outside.

'Woof, woof . . .' he said. The call went unanswered. Russell was becoming a little nervous. There was a single moment when he thought – Mick! Was his brother back, trying to pick up where they had left off?

Suddenly, a hand snatched at his arm, pulling him back towards the doorway of the boiler room. He fought back, but his attacker was too strong. He found himself pinned against the door, his arm trapped up his back. He winced and closed his eyes against the pain.

'Great minds think alike, eh?' hissed an accented voice.

'Jace?'

'Who else? A nice touch that, hiding up in the pipes. Me,

I wouldn't have wanted to be caught behind the fence though. I like to have room to move.'

'Jace,' Russ gasped, 'we were looking for you!'

The grip on his arm relaxed a little, so that the worst of the discomfort subsided.

'I know,' said Jace, 'I saw you and Chris talking earlier with the others. I watched you slip off and then some other kids started hanging around outside the hall, running fifteen minute shifts.'

'You saw all that?'

'Sure. I've been here all day. Seemed like the one place I knew that would be quiet, it being the holidays and all.'

'Chris figured you'd try to make contact tonight – look, all we really want to do is help.'

'Well, right now, it's not me that needs help.'

Russell felt the arm lock loosen off even more. He turned slightly so that he could see Jace's face for the first time. The American looked extremely serious.

'What do you mean?'

'Chris is in big trouble. Get some of the other guys and bring them over behind the gym.'

'Where will you be?'

Jace grinned and winked as he turned away. 'Where do you think?' he asked.

'What are you prats doing here?' Chris asked, showing little sign of a strong sense of self-preservation. It wasn't even a question he wanted to hear the answer to.

The nearest of the other boys, the same one who had jumped up in front of Chris from behind the wall, pressed his ugly, twisted face closer to Chris's, so close that their noses were touching. The kid's breath stank of stale food. Chris would have turned away, but he was held fast from behind by one of Ugly's mates.

'Well,' the boy sneered, with a small, smug look around at his six compatriots, 'we were hoping to find some loud-mouthed jerk from Spirebrook so we could give him a kicking. Looks like we'll have to make do with you.'

This, thought Chris, is not part of the plan.

'What's your problem?' demanded Chris, struggling against the tight grasp of the two boys behind him. They forced him to bend forward, stretching his arms back and up. One of them locked his fingers into Chris's hair.

'We don't have a problem,' Ugly jeered. 'You do.'

Two snappy comebacks in two questions, Chris thought to himself. Just his luck to come up against the biggest comedian at Blackmoor Comprehensive.

He had no doubt that that was where this lot were from. Even in the dark, he was sure he recognised a couple of them from other run-ins. Blackmoor and Spirebrook didn't like each other and Chris had been involved in a few sparring matches with kids from the other school before.

Ugly was gripping his jacket. They always seemed to do that, in Chris's experience of run-ins with Blackmoor's students. Perhaps it was on the curriculum there. It appeared this bunch had turned up to the disco on the off-chance they could cause some trouble. They had been loitering round by the rubbish bins and Chris had wandered right into them.

'I only have to call, and you guys will be in *big* trouble . . .' said Chris, wishing hard that it was true.

'Who's going to hear you over that music?' Ugly said confidently. 'Besides, you're not gonna say nothing, not unless you want my fist in your mouth.'

A short kid with greasy black hair, standing at Ugly's shoulder, piped up: 'What shall we do with him, Kev?' He had a thin, high-pitched voice. Even Ugly winced at the sound of it.

'We've got what we came for,' Ugly sneered. 'Let's take him for a swimming lesson in the river!'

The others cheered their agreement and the two kids behind Chris started to turn him so they could frogmarch him across the school grounds to the back gate.

Which was when everyone realised that someone was blocking the way.

'Actually,' Jace said, 'Chris swims pretty well. He's got a 50 metre certificate on the wall in his bedroom.'

The guys from Blackmoor took a moment to recalculate the odds. It wasn't a skinny wimp who had appeared in front of them, but there were still six or seven of them and just two of the good guys. Although the Blackmorons would find the maths hard, they were still winning the numbers game.

Ugly, who had been behind Chris when Jace appeared, pushed through to the front.

'I don't know you,' he snarled. 'You're not a "Brooker".'

'Correct,' replied Jace.

'You're not even English!' Ugly cried. 'You're a Yank.'

'I can see how you got to be team leader,' Jace said, still smiling.

'This isn't any of your business,' Ugly whispered threateningly. 'I suggest you keep your nose out of stuff that doesn't concern you.'

Jace held up his hands as if he understood. 'I agree,' he said. 'No point getting involved in some kind of school rivalry thing. That is what this thing is, right?'

Ugly looked as if he could smell something unpleasant. It was probably his own breath.

'Maybe . . .' he said.

'That's what I thought,' Jace continued, still looking completely innocent. 'I heard about these fights between your British schools. You guys must be from some other school, right?'

Ugly nodded.

'And you got this thing against guys from Spirebrook, right?'

Another nod.

'Good for you!' said Jace, grinning. 'I can't stand them either. They really think they're hot, you know? You should hear them! The way they talk about kids from other schools! It's really sick.'

The black-haired weasel with the voice like radio static walked into the trap like a lemming heading for a cliff.

'Like what?'

Jace rubbed his chin as if he was trying to remember. 'Well, there's this one school, right, that they seem to have it in for real bad. They told me that there were plans to build a pig farm near this other school, but the plans were dropped on account of complaints about the smell – from the pigs. Then I heard tell how this other school was going to be bulldozed to make way for a land fill site, until they realised it was a rubbish dump already . . .'

Chris felt the grip on his arms tighten and hideous growls were coming from several of the Blackmoor kids' mouths. Jace had worked them up into a spiteful rage; all he had to do now was ignite it and they would be after him like a hurricane. Chris – even through his pain – managed a small smile. Jace was paying him back for the incident in the dressing room.

'So, what are you doing with them?' asked Ugly.

'Me? I don't have any choice. I'm here on an exchange visit. In just over a week, I get to go home to the USA. It can't happen soon enough for me.'

There was a long pause then, while the guys from Blackmoor looked at each other, clearly not certain whose side the stranger was on or what he was hoping to achieve.

Do it now! Chris thought, and he looked up to meet Jace's steady gaze. The silence extended even further. Chris could feel his heart hammering in his chest and beads of sweat on his brow and palms. Do it *now*!

'Still, I'd better not keep you any longer,' Jace said at last, and he moved off the path as if to let them through.

Chris's mouth fell open. 'What?!' he gasped.

One of the boys standing at his side swung round and drove his fist hard into Chris's stomach, doubling him up. He spat on to the floor, trying hard to draw breath back into his lungs.

'Keep your gob shut,' the boy said. Chris fell silent – not so much through choice as necessity.

Jace was concentrating on talking to Ugly. 'I'd better be going. There are some people looking for me who I'd rather not meet up with. Not to mention that things are bound to get a little crazy when the idiots here discover you've tied one of their mates naked to the wall bars in the gym.'

'Hey!' giggled Squeaky Voice. 'Neat idea!'

'We're dumping him in the river!' snapped Ugly.

'Why bother?' Jace continued. 'It's a long walk and the gate's locked so you'll have to get him through the fence somehow –'

'We hadn't thought of that,' squealed Squeaky-Voice.

'Yes I had!' Ugly argued, although he didn't go out of his

way to explain what solution he had dreamed up to the rest of his gang. 'But maybe the gym is a better plan. We could find some paint, maybe . . .'

The rest of his posse were laughing and making other suggestions, some of which sent a shiver up Chris's spine. Throughout, though, he kept his eyes locked on Jace Goodman. Some small part of him was still hoping this was a plan to distract the gang somehow, until Jace launched himself into the attack. The rest of him was starting to wonder just how he'd get even.

'Jace!' he snarled. Goodman looked towards him for the first time in several minutes. 'I'll get even with you for this . . .'

'Oh, get real, Stephens. What were you expecting, that I'd go up against seven guys just for you?' He laughed dryly, then his face hardened. 'Listen, you know the score, Stephens. I don't have time to hang around here.'

With that, he started to move back off the path. Chris felt the boys behind him start to propel him forward once again. His arms felt like they were being wrenched out of their sockets. A stinging jolt of pain brought tears to Chris's eyes. Inside, he felt a fierce anger start to burn. If he got out of this, he was going to repay Jace for tonight.

'One more thing,' Jace called as they were about to pass by. 'There's a window on the upper floor; it leads into the bathroom. It's been open all night. That's how you get in.'

'Thanks!' screeched Squeaky Voice. He giggled loudly, then tried to stifle it with his hands.

'Remember,' Jace repeated, emphasising the words even more carefully. 'Bathroom window; upstairs; open all night.'

The gang rushed on, quickly passing the spot where Jace had been standing. Chris turned his head as much as he was able, but he couldn't see Jace at all. It was as if the American had melted into the shadows.

Chris tried to stay loose, running at the same pace as they did, trying to avoid his arms being wrenched any further than they were. They hurried past the main doors and scampered over the playground.

No-one saw them; no-one interrupted their progress at all. They moved swiftly into the shadows beside the gym, following it round towards the back. Ugly was grinning madly, as if he was still sorting through the list of what they'd do to Chris once they got him inside.

'Hey –' Squeaky Voice called, as they reached the far corner.

'What is it?' Ugly snarled, looking back over his shoulder.

'Is this the right building?'

The group slowed down. Several of them looked back to where Squeaky had halted, and followed his gaze up to the top of the gym, wondering what was troubling him.

At the front of the group, Ugly had stopped at the corner of the building. 'Of course it is! You've been here before. Right at the end, by the sports field, with bike racks at the back.' He gestured towards the roughly built shed at the rear of the building, where the empty aluminium frames were just visible in the darkness. He froze.

'Yeah, but this is just a single-storey building,' Squeaky Voice continued, unaware that his audience was no longer paying attention. 'That American kid said –'

He turned to face the others, aware of a growing rustle and the approaching rush of feet. At once, he realised why no-one was that interested in the number of floors the gym had. From every side, large numbers of Spirebrook students were closing in on them. One of them had a wide, white-toothed grin on his face and he walked forward with great eagerness.

'Boy, have you guys made a mistake,' said Nicky, as he reached out to grab Squeaky . . .

⚽

'We should have more discos like that,' said Fuller, loud enough for everyone to hear, including Mrs Cole, Spirebrook's head teacher. She shot him a warning glance that Fuller missed completely. He was in far too good a mood to worry about possible punishment after the holidays.

Chris leaned back in his chair, blinking against the glare of the bright hall lights. As he stretched, he felt a twinge along the side of his chest which suggested he was in for a bruise there. He was also aware of how his shoulders ached from having been twisted for so long.

Nicky nudged him in the ribs, which made him wince. He turned to face his mate – who was completely unblemished.

'Did you see how Fuller got that black eye?'

'No. In case you didn't notice, I was a little preoccupied.' Grateful though he was for the rescue, Chris hadn't appreciated being used as a shield in the first rush. A couple of his mates had almost run over him in their impatience to get at the invaders from Blackmoor.

'One of the Yanks gave it to him! Couldn't tell one side from the other, so when he saw Fuller, he walloped him!'

'You sure it was an accident?' observed Chris.

The sarcasm in Chris's voice was wasted on Nicky, who was still bubbling about the fight. Several of the Blackmoor gang had been three years older than them, which more or less balanced out the numbers advantage in Nicky's eyes. The way he was starting to tell it, the fight had been even more heroic than either Trafalgar, Agincourt or the Battle of Britain, and a greater victory than all three rolled into one.

Naturally, Nicky had gone one on one with the 'biggest of the lot', which wasn't how Chris would have described Squeaky Voice, but still . . .

'Yeah! Didn't you see? Some of the Yanks really came through for us! Even Mason Williams got stuck in and he's not exactly your biggest fan.'

The Americans were sitting in a small group to one side, getting a stern lecture from Mr Carter, which involved words like 'ashamed', 'letting your country down' and 'what would your parents say?'. Chris watched them carefully as he searched through their ranks to make sure Jace wasn't there. They didn't look as if their parents' opinions were the most important things on their minds. The only ones who looked fed up were those who hadn't been able to take part.

Jazz, who was sitting behind them, leaned forward. He had a plaster on his forehead and looked very, very uncomfortable.

'Do you think they'll let us go home soon?' he asked.

'Yeah, yeah,' snapped Nicky. 'You'll be able to go and explain it all to your dad soon enough.'

'That's what I was afraid of,' Jazz confessed as he sat back. 'I think I'd prefer it if they kept us here all night.'

That last phrase made Chris jump. He suddenly realised just how late it could be getting (his watch was broken; something he was trying not to think about). He wanted to get back home.

'Ms Robinson, are we going to be leaving soon?'

The geography teacher, who had been pacing back and forth in front of them like she was on guard duty, stopped and faced Chris, with a stern, angry look on her face.

'What's the matter, Stephens? Got another fight to get to?'

Chris resisted the temptation to make a witty remark in reply. He got the impression that Ms Robinson would not be the best recipient of his humour at the moment. As one of the youngest teachers, she had been drafted in by Mrs Cole to help the evening pass off successfully. Instead, she had found herself forced to try and separate the participants in a wild brawl over by the gym. Never mind that for the likes of Nicky, the brawl had made the disco the most successful there had ever been. Her evening had not gone as planned.

'No, Mi –' Chris muttered (what were you supposed to do when you just wanted to use the 'Ms' part of 'Ms Robinson'; just saying 'Ms' sounded like you were doing an impersonation of an insect).

'Well?' she demanded, looking very flushed and angry.

'My father will be getting worried,' Chris replied lamely.

'From what I see he has plenty to worry about!' she cried. 'But I don't think you have too much to worry about. It's only 9.30. If you hadn't been more interested in behaving like hooligans, the disco would still be going!'

Chris looked around the hall. Nearly everyone else had gone, except for a giggling batch of girls sitting in the corner who were waiting for lifts. The DJ was packing away his equipment, having barely had time to warm up his amplifier before proceedings had been brought to a halt. 'Flea' was transporting the combatants from Blackmoor back to their home turf. That just left the dozen or so who had taken part on their side.

Ms Robinson went back to her pacing, lengthening the route to bring her a little closer to Mrs Cole, who was deep in conversation with Sean Priest and Stefan Brodenberg. Chris wished he could read lips. Stefan looked very tense, keeping half an eye on Mr Carter and also shooting the occasional glance in Chris's direction. Priest was nodding thoughtfully, listening carefully to everything Mrs Cole said.

'On a scale of ten, how much trouble would you say we were in?' asked Nicky, who was watching in the same direction.

'Sixteen,' said Jazz from behind.

They ignored him.

'Nine,' said Chris. 'You know how Andy Cole can be when she thinks sport is getting in the way of other things.'

Mrs Cole tended to accept the need for competitive teams at Spirebrook only very grudgingly. No-one played for the school who didn't also have an excellent disciplinary and academic record. Chris could remember her warning him about his behaviour once and almost taking him off the soccer team. Nicky had always cut things pretty fine too.

'Nah, strictly a six,' Nicky insisted. 'The Blackmoor kids were out of order, invading our territory like that.' Chris grinned at Nicky's adoption of words right out of a story about LA gangs. It was particularly funny hearing him call school 'our territory'. 'I bet I'm right,' Nicky continued in a hurt tone, having caught Chris covering up his chuckle. 'This was a home fixture; she'll see it's their fault and that we were just defending ourselves.'

'Nicky, what she'll see is that twenty of us went steaming into seven of them. She'll say we should have told the staff there was a problem and let them deal with it.'

They both knew this was just the sort of nonsense a head teacher would believe.

'OK, maybe a seven, then. A nine for you, though, because you're captain of the football team.'

Before Chris could respond to that, there was movement behind them. Someone was swapping places with Phil Lucas, who played up front with Chris for the school team.

'Woof, woof,' came a voice.

'Bow, wow!' Chris and Nicky replied together, trying hard not to let Ms Robinson catch them giggling. Nicky was insanely proud of his code words and his enthusiasm was catching.

'What do you think's going on?' asked Russell, leaning

forward over Chris's shoulder to observe the animated discussions among the adults.

'Who knows?' said Chris. 'But I bet we're not about to win any prizes for good behaviour.'

'They can't give us detention,' observed Nicky. 'Not during Easter.'

Chris wasn't so sure. Mrs Cole looked angry enough to lock them all in school with Mr Stewart, the world's most boring history teacher.

'It's not fair,' muttered Nicky. 'Blackmoor were to blame.'

Russell was watching the Americans. Eleven unhappy faces – the guilty and the innocent – looked up as Mr Carter continued his lecture.

'Where's Jace?' he asked after a while.

'Jace?' asked Nicky, who had become very jumpy at the sound of that name, convinced that everyone knew that he was part of the guilty conspiracy to hide Jace from the world. 'Why would he be with them? He didn't come to the disco.' He shot a nervous glance at Chris, who realised that he still hadn't had the chance to explain to Nicky what had happened outside before the rescue party had been summoned.

'But you were right, he did come looking for Chris,' said Russell. 'It was him who told me that Chris was in trouble and got me to fetch help. Said he'd been hiding here all day.'

Nicky looked at Chris anxiously, clearly wondering if their plans had been uncovered. They'd had to let Russ, Jazz and a few others in on *part* of the secret, so they could all keep an eye out for Jace that evening, but they hadn't told anyone why Jace had run off – just that he might try to make contact with them while the disco was on.

'Did you see him?' Nicky asked Chris.

'Yes, briefly,' Chris replied.

Nicky narrowed his eyes and stared across the hall as well. Chris heard him counting, stopping at eleven.

'He's not with them . . .' Nicky reported. Chris had already noticed that for himself.

'He's pretty sneaky,' Russell said admiringly. 'I thought I was really well hidden, but he spotted me right away. He told me you were in trouble and that I should get the rest of the guys to head round the back of the gym. Then he ran off – I thought he was coming to lend you a hand, Chris.'

Russell's explanation cleared up how the lads from Spirebrook (with some help from the American contingent) had managed to find Chris so quickly. Chris smiled secretly.

'Did he?' Nicky was asking, and Chris had to stop and think what Nicky was asking about.

'Yes, sort of. He stalled them for a while, to give Russ time to get the rest of you. Then he tricked them into heading for the gym.' Chris could only admire the way Jace had done it, still managing to slip away before the real trouble started.

'So where is he now?' moaned Nicky. 'I hope we haven't gone to all this trouble for nothing.'

Chris's smile broadened still wider. 'Don't worry,' he said. 'I've just worked out how he's going to get in touch again. And when he does, I have a plan of my own, so that we don't have to go through this kind of hassle again.'

Nicky looked at Chris with a suspicious glint in his eye. Chris's plans were rarely simple. The fact that they usually worked didn't mean they were any easier to understand.

'You've got somewhere in mind where Jace can stay hidden?'

'Uh-huh,' Chris replied, and it was getting hard not to laugh. 'We're going to hide him in the last place anyone will look. All I need is a little help from you guys . . . and maybe Sean Priest . . .'

Nine

Chris went up to his room shortly after he got home, although sleep was the last thing on his mind. Bearing in mind everything that had happened that day, he was tired, but his mind was buzzing with memories of the events and his plan to rescue Jace from . . . whatever it was.

It still irritated Chris that Jace hadn't confided in him, but in the light of the way Jace had handled the incident with the guys from Blackmoor, Chris felt he just had to trust the American and do what he could to help. He felt a strange excited buzz in the pit of his stomach at the prospect of trying to get to the bottom of this mystery.

He powered up the computer and checked for any more e-mail. Nothing. Leaving it running, but with the monitor turned off so that no light showed, he went to the bathroom and cleaned his teeth, making sure to leave the window unlocked. After that, all he could do was wait.

He heard his father go to bed at about 11.30pm. Fortunately, he didn't know anything of what had occurred that night – Mrs Cole had decided to postpone making any decision about punishment until after Easter. From what Chris could tell, Sean Priest had tried to get her to accept that the battle with the lads from Blackmoor wasn't anything to do with the football team, so Chris didn't feel that he was going to be singled out for punishment. Mrs Cole had no idea that Chris had actually been ambushed before the main fight – she just assumed that a group from Spirebrook had gone after the Blackmorons when they'd been discovered sneaking around the school.

Which was close enough to the truth so that no-one needed to tell her any different.

Chris wasn't able to manage the same kind of trick with his father, however. He'd had to tell him that Jace was staying the night with one of the other Americans. He'd hidden Jace's jacket and a few other things in his room when he'd returned from his jaunt into the city with Nicky. Chris knew his father was a bit suspicious about this story, but he hadn't challenged it yet.

He wondered whether he should confide in his father, but he knew his dad would want to report it to the police. Chris couldn't do that without admitting that he had let the bogus US government man into the house.

That was a mistake he wasn't ready to admit to just yet.

There were all kinds of other traps waiting to trip him up as well. He'd told Benford Carter that Jace was at home; that he hadn't wanted to go to the disco. He hadn't wanted Mr Carter to be worried, but it was a flimsy story at best.

The clock beside his bed glowed brightly in the darkened room, counting off the seconds with the steady pulse of its LEDs. Chris sat on his bed, listening to the traffic outside, wondering if any of the other night sounds might be Ripley or the sinister Mr Jackson, prowling round the house. Chris had no doubt that anyone wanting to catch Jace would keep a watch on the place. Would Jace be able to evade them?

The minutes ticked on, becoming first one hour, then two. Chris felt fatigue catching up with him and he twice caught himself nodding off.

He tried to fight it, but he was actually more asleep than awake when a hand closed over his mouth and a voice ordered him to be silent.

He could just about make out that the shape moving in the dark was Jace. Chris nodded to show that he knew who it was and Jace released his grip.

'I didn't hear you come in,' Chris acknowledged.

'I can be pretty sneaky,' said Jace, smiling. 'I've had a lot of practice.'

'What took you so long?'

Jace was kneeling on the end of the bed, touching back the corner of the curtain to look through a narrow chink at the street below. Chris rubbed his eyes and dragged his fingers through his unruly hair, trying to wake up fully.

'The house is being watched. There's a car just along the way. I couldn't get close enough to see who was in it. I had to be careful in case they had anyone out the back.'

'What kind of car was it?' asked Chris.

Jace looked at him sharply, as if wondering what possible difference it could make. 'A sports car of some kind . . .'

Chris figured he knew who that meant. 'Two guys were here earlier. One of them said he was your father; the other said his name was Jackson.'

The second name didn't mean anything to Jace. He asked for a description of the first man and his eyes brightened when Chris gave it to him.

'That could be my dad,' he said. 'But it doesn't make sense. What would he be doing here in England?'

'Looking for you?' asked Chris, even though it was stating the obvious. Jace's face had quickly become quite miserable.

'You don't understand,' he muttered. 'He shouldn't be here at all . . .'

Chris waited, wondering if Jace might be about to explain the whole deal at last, but the American wasn't ready yet.

'I need to use the computer,' he said instead, moving from the bed to the desk.

'It's already on,' said Chris. 'Just switch on the monitor.' He watched as Jace was illuminated by the growing glow of the screen. 'I've already looked to see if there was any e-mail today,' Chris added.

'I'm not expecting any more,' Jace said softly. He adjusted the screen's brightness so that it was as low as it could be without everything becoming unreadable.

Chris remained where he was sitting, knowing that Jace was opening the system folder, searching for the e-mail file he had stashed there that morning. As he watched, Jace became quite agitated, scrolling back and forth through the folder.

'It's not here!' he gasped.

Chris was every bit as amazed. 'It must be!' he said, getting up and going over to look over Jace's shoulder.

'I put it in here before I sneaked out this morning,' Jace told Chris.

'I know,' Chris replied automatically. He realised his mistake as soon as it was too late. Jace looked up at him, frowning. 'I –

uh – was just seeing what it was,' Chris explained, lamely.

'Did you read it?'

Chris hesitated. Technically, perhaps, he could answer 'no', since he'd actually read it later. Not wanting to get caught in such a clumsy piece of self-justification, however, he opted for avoiding the question.

'I copied it.'

He took the mouse from Jace's hand and opened up the folder in which he had stashed the duplicate. He stepped back to allow Jace to open the file, even though he had committed the words to memory before.

Jace's lips moved as he read the short message. He didn't say anything for a long while afterwards. When Chris went back to stand beside him, he could see Jace had been crying silently.

'What is it?'

'My mum's alive . . .' said Jace, the words sounding more like small sobs. He looked up at Chris. 'I know this is going to sound crazy, but for the last month I haven't been sure one way or the other.'

Chris said nothing, wondering if Jace would be prepared to say any more. Instead, the American wiped his eyes, sniffed and closed the file. When he next spoke, his voice, though soft, was as controlled as ever.

'They must have seen the e-mail I sent to my dad's office on the off-chance that he wasn't a prisoner,' Jace said, more to himself than to Chris. He turned round to face Chris. 'You copied the file?'

'Yes,' whispered Chris.

'You didn't delete the original?'

'No.' And Chris was confident enough about how the Mac worked to know that it wasn't likely to have happened accidentally.

'You know what this means, then?' Jace said.

Chris did, though he chose not to reply. He looked around the room for any other tell-tale sign that anyone had been in. There was nothing.

Jace's mind was obviously thinking along the same lines. He crept out of Chris's room and stole along the landing to the guest bedroom.

Chris waited in his own room. He switched off the computer, then took a moment to copy what Jace had done earlier and peek out through a crack between the curtains at the darkened street outside. There was no sign of any car that didn't belong there – certainly there was no sign of the sports car Mr Goodman and his ominous companion used.

Jace reappeared, looking anxious and ill at ease. He'd picked up his jacket, baseball cap and backpack. Chris saw there were a few clothes stuffed hurriedly into the latter.

'My room's been searched.'

'Ripley did that when he found you were gone,' said Chris.

Jace's expression was fixed as he considered this. 'Did he take anything?' he asked.

'Not that I saw,' Chris replied.

'Then someone else has been here. They took the camera my father bought me for Christmas.' He sounded really upset at the news.

Chris tried to think if Ripley had had time to remove it. He was sure he hadn't. That meant the house had been entered while he and Nicky had been out at lunchtime, with Sean and Stefan. But who by?

'Why would anyone want that?' asked Chris. From what he could remember, it was an ordinary 35mm compact. Nice, but nothing amazing.

'The film . . .' gasped Jace, who had clearly only just worked it out himself.

'What?'

'I took the film out of the camera . . .' He crept out of the room again quickly and this time Chris followed. Instead of heading for the back bedroom, though, he went into the kitchen. The film was just where he had left it, on the shelf with the tea and coffee jars. He closed his fist around it.

'What's so special about that?' Chris asked. Jace went to the kitchen cupboard and took out an unopened jar of Kenco from inside. He unscrewed the lid, broke the seal, and poured some of the coffee into the opened jar on the kitchen shelf. Then he put the film inside the new jar, shook it up so the film was invisible among the granules, then put it back in the cupboard. Still having avoided giving an answer, Jace stepped lightly back across the kitchen and climbed the stairs once more.

By the time he had reached the bedroom as well, Chris was fuming. Just what was Jace playing at? He wanted to shout at him and let him know just how sick he was of his closed-mouthed silence about his past. Instead, knowing that his father was sleeping just a few metres away, he was forced to utter his angry questions in a brisk, harsh whisper.

'What is it with you, Jace? Why won't you let me help you?'

'You can't!' Jace insisted.

'What's on that film?' Chris had only seen Jace use the camera once, on that first tour round the city, when Jace had sat sullenly on the bus for the whole day, except when he had observed some horses in a field. He had stepped off the coach while his team mates were busy hunting for souvenirs and taken a couple of snaps of the two old nags before they had wandered over in response to his call. He had fed them an apple he had in his backpack and spoken with them – pretty much the first words Chris had heard him speak voluntarily. Whatever was so important about that film, Chris knew it wasn't a couple of bored gee-gees.

'I don't know,' Jace replied. He was stuffing his clothes more securely into his backpack.

Chris almost slapped Jace around the back of the head, he was so fed up with the American's evasion.

'Don't give me that! You must know! Why else is it so important to you?'

Jace signalled at Chris to drop his voice. Chris tried to do so, but his frustration with Jace was boiling over. This was worse than arguing with Nicky!

'I can't tell you what's on the film because I don't know,' said Jace. 'My father borrowed the camera the last time I saw him – weeks ago. He must have left a film in it. When I took those couple of shots at the beginning of the week, I used up the last of it. I bought a new film in the gift shop and loaded it in instead.'

Chris froze, unable to think of anything to say now that Jace's explanation had turned out to be so reasonable.

'But there must be something important on it,' he said,

finally recovering his wits. 'Or why else would someone have tried to steal it?'

Jace shrugged and Chris realised that Jace wasn't going to help by indulging in any guesswork.

'Why don't we just get the film developed?' asked Chris. It seemed like the only logical step.

'I can't,' Jace insisted. 'You've got to promise me that you'll leave it in the jar until I come back.'

Chris sat down beside Jace's pack. 'That's stupid! If we get the pictures, we'll know what's going on . . .'

'Maybe I don't want to know,' whispered Jace.

Chris grabbed his arm. 'You can trust me, you know,' he said, desperate to get Jace to open up. No matter how much trouble Jace might be in, Chris wanted him to know he was on his side.

'Like I could trust you not to read my e-mail?' asked Jace. It was only a lucky guess, of course, but it hit the target perfectly. Chris sighed in defeat. It took him another moment or two to realise just what Jace had said before.

'Hang on – get back from where?'

'I can't stay here, Chris. Sooner or later I'm going to get caught.'

'But where will you go?'

Jace shrugged. Chris realised Jace didn't have any kind of plan in mind; he just knew he had to escape.

'You can't keep running from your problems, Jace.'

'No? It's worked so far,' Jace replied, with real bitterness in his voice. Then he added sadly, 'I just need some time to think.'

'OK,' said Chris, 'but you won't get any thinking done while you're dodging. You're not in America now, Jace, and you can't get back – I know you came over on Benford's passport. Besides, what would you use for money? Face it, you're stuck here.'

'So what? The people looking for me don't know the country any better than I do. I'll still be able to avoid them.'

'That's true,' Chris said, 'but they can ask for help and you can't. They could start the police looking for you, or hire somebody to find you. You can't. You don't know anybody and you don't have any friends who can help you – except for me and Nicky.'

'Your Italian mate?' asked Jace. 'What's he got to do with it? You're not suggesting I stay at his house? They're bound to look for me there.'

'They won't find you,' said Chris. 'They'll find someone else.'

The time had come to let Jace hear The Plan.

Sunday dawned, bright and warm. There was a light southerly wind and the sun climbed into a sky patched only intermittently by puffs of white cloud.

It was a perfect spring day for a game of football.

Chris, for whom a dank, wet November day was equally perfect when there was a match to be played, ran on to the grass of Cathedral's home pitch, breathing deeply. He stretched out his leg muscles, practised a few leaps into the air, then trapped a ball Jazz passed along the ground.

If the Colts won this match, they were Champions. That alone made it a game to look forward to, especially since Cathedral were by no means the most formidable team in the Oldcester District Youth League. Rory, Stamp, Tollie and the others were geeing each other up, telling themselves that after today they could relax with the trophy in the bag.

For Chris, though, the game had an added significance. It was the first test of The Plan.

He played the ball back to Jazz and looked around. There weren't too many people there to watch the game, which was being played on one of the council's pitches in a part of the city called St Paul's. Certainly nobody you wouldn't expect to see; a few parents and other supporters for Cathedral; a slightly larger contingent to see if Riverside were going to win the Championship; two or three passers-by.

But there were other pitches – twenty of them – dotted all over St Paul's Fields, with other spectators watching them. Chris couldn't see Ripley, Mr Goodman, the sinister Mr Jackson, or anyone connected with the exchange, but that didn't mean they weren't out there somewhere.

The ball returned to him, hip-high. Chris stepped across, trapped it on his thigh, then caught the ball on his instep as it fell. He flicked it back up, stroking the ball towards one of his team mates, who was warming up rather erratically on the touchline.

'Jimmy!' he called, as he hit the ball.

Jimmy looked up, to find a pin-point pass landing at his boots. He stuck out a foot but misjudged the flight of the ball, which skidded under his boot. With a nervous and apologetic yelp, he went off after it.

'Oh, yes, this is going to work brilliantly,' sighed Jazz.

Chris turned and gestured at Jazz to keep his opinions to himself. He continued his warm-up exercises, which carried him closer to where Jimmy was running back with the ball under his arm.

'Use your feet!' hissed Chris.

Jimmy dropped the ball, reacting so quickly it was almost as if the ball was red hot. The ball ran away in front of him and he chased after it quickly. Chris could see just how nervous he was and tried hard to encourage the Colts' new player.

'Hit a pass to Rory,' he advised. 'Just stroke the ball gently with the inside of the boot and follow through.'

Jimmy hit the pass. It was nice and solid, but it landed directly at Polly's feet, some eight or nine metres to Rory's right.

'Spread your arms for balance,' Chris told him. 'Look, watch me . . .'

For what seemed like the thousandth time, Chris showed Jimmy how to kick a football so that it landed at least approximately close to the target. Head down, over the ball; draw your foot back, follow through after contact. Chris's pass drilled twenty metres, landing at Rory's side.

Jimmy nodded. Chris couldn't see his face, but he knew his new team mate would be pale and sweating under the hood of his training top.

'Take the hood down, Jace,' he whispered. 'You look a berk.'

He tried not to stare as 'Jimmy' lowered the hood. The boy's face was fixed in a wide-eyed, fear-filled stare. He touched his jet-black hair back from his forehead, looking quite self-conscious and ill at ease. Chris gave him an 'it looks fine' wink and turned to call for a return pass from Rory.

'This is never going to work,' he heard Jace moan. He

seemed to pull at his body as if he was wearing an itchy vest.

Chris collected the ball, picked it up and went back over to Jace so that they could go through some stretching exercises.

'Leave the padding alone! And keep calm, OK? It's not as if you've got to play or anything. You just have to look like you're one of the subs.'

'This is dumb!' Jace said in a louder voice, clearly not convinced. Chris winced as the American's accent echoed across the field.

'Keep your voice down!' warned Chris, trying to look as natural and normal as possible.

Jace growled unhappily, helping Chris stretch out his hamstrings.

'I can't believe I agreed to this. It isn't even going to work! No-one is going to be fooled by this disguise.'

They had been over this several times already, Chris thought, ever since he and Jace had stolen round to Nicky's house early the morning after the disco to begin Phase One of The Plan. Natalie – Nicky's cousin – had spent hours working on disguising Jace's appearance. His hair was now the same jet black as any of the Fiorentinis; his skin colour had been darkened to the same olive tone as theirs; his eyebrows were thicker and she had even managed to make the shape of his face look different somehow.

The biggest trick had been in disguising Jace's size. He was distinctively broad at the shoulder, but Natalie had brought something that looked like a padded shirt home from the costume department of the TV company where she worked, which made Jace look heavier all over.

From a distance, he looked completely different. Chris wanted to believe it might even fool someone who knew Jace quite well – even though he would stick out like a lighthouse among the rest of the Colts team, with the possible exception of Rory Blackstone.

Perhaps they should have disguised him as 'Jimmy Blackstone'.

Chris kept calm and put a broad smile on his face as he replied. 'Look, we both know this is your only chance. Everyone who's looking for you knows you've rumbled them; if you stayed at my place they'd make sure there was no back way out next time. As for running round Spirebrook like a wild animal, how long could you keep that up?'

'Hey, man, I managed to hike across the USA on my own – and they were looking for me then!'

Chris sighed. Jace was so confident in his own abilities, he was hard to reason with. He had already told the story (several times over) of how he had escaped from the guys who had ambushed him at the Pacific campsite, climbed back up to the main road and hitchhiked to LA (only he had left out all the details about what had happened to his mother). From there, Chris knew, Jace had called his uncle and begun the long journey across the States to New Jersey.

'This isn't the USA, Jace, it's England. When you hitchhiked to LA, people believed your story; who's going to believe you if you try telling people in England that your buddies left you on the beach as a practical joke?'

'Well, I wouldn't use the same story, would I? I'm not that dumb!'

'Not quite,' muttered Chris. He took a deep breath, and allowed the argument to go on. 'It wouldn't matter what story you used. It wouldn't sound right over here. You're a Yank; people are going to hear that accent and know that you don't belong here on your own. They'll ask questions; maybe call the police. And they'll call the US embassy. If Ripley is some kind of government agent, he'll hear about it as soon as you surface.'

Jace looked as if he had some new point to make about that, so Chris quickly jumped in and continued the familiar demolition of Jace's objections.

'And remember, last time you were able to wire your uncle and get him to send you the money for your plane ticket. That isn't an option this time, is it?'

'I guess not . . .'

'Right. We're sure they'll be watching your uncle, waiting for you to make contact. If they've tracked you down this far, they must know that you came over on Benford's passport, pretending to be his kid. They'll know you can't get back without Benford's help.'

Jace was starting to look miserable. Having Chris spell out the cold hard facts wasn't comforting.

'You don't have any real friends in the rest of the team, so you can't call on them to help you out either. So, all we can do is find a different way of hiding you so that these creeps who are looking for you don't see you. This is the best way.'

'You call this hiding? Dressing me up in a bright red and blue costume like Spiderman and making me run round a field?'

'I can't imagine that anyone who knows you would look for you on a soccer pitch, Jace. If they do happen to look this way, all they'll see is Jimmy, Nicky's cousin from Cambridge who's come to live in Oldcester, who's signed for the Colts and who's covering for Nixon while he goes off on holiday over Easter.' The cover story, at least, sounded fairly convincing, at least to Chris. No-one had challenged it yet.

Jimmy looked round, making the same inspection of the spectators that Chris had. He lingered longest on the figure of Iain Walsh, who was staring hard at the pair of them.

'So, who knows about this plan?'

'Me, Nicky, Russ, Jazz and Sean Priest.' He saw where Jace was watching. 'Iain doesn't know anything about it; he just thinks Sean found you through Nicky. He knows the Fiorentinis have hundreds of cousins and that some of them play football. So far, he's accepted the story without any problem.' How long that would last if Walsh had a chance to see just how well 'Jimmy' could play was a problem Chris didn't want to face just yet.

There had been plenty of other problems to deal with. Chris had told his father that Jace had gone to stay with another family since he and Chris obviously didn't get on. That, at least, was close to being true.

Benford Carter, though, was frantic with worry, and it wasn't going to be easy to keep him calm, even though Jace had phoned twice to tell him that he was OK and just keeping out of sight. It was a miracle he hadn't called the police already.

The easy part of the plan had been getting Nicky's family involved. They had been sold it as being a practical gag, and had thrown themselves into helping make it work. Only Uncle Fabian knew parts of the real story – just enough to ensure his help. The others accepted Jace into the family, so much so that Nicky's aged grandmother actually believed he was a cousin she'd forgotten about.

Jace continued to stare towards the sidelines. Chris tapped him on the shoulder to make him focus on the more immediate problem.

'None of this will work if you don't make a passable effort to look like you belong. That's why we were practising all day yesterday! So, come on, try another pass.'

He backed away, drawing the ball back under his heel. From a distance of no more than three metres, he hit a side-foot pass towards Jace's stronger right foot. It was gentle and predictable and this time Jace managed to trap the ball and even make a reasonable return. Maybe all the time Chris and Nicky had spent with him was paying off.

They exchanged another couple of passes, with Chris gradually increasing the distance between them. By staying alert and reacting quickly, he was able to make Jace's more wayward passes look more convincing. Even so, it was a relief when the ref signalled that he was ready to start.

'Just hang around with the other subs,' Chris told him as Jace turned to leave the field. 'Stay at the back.'

'I just hope Iain doesn't decide to bring me on!'

Chris was dreading the same thing, but he didn't think it likely. Iain Walsh looked far from impressed with their new 'star' player.

⚽

With eleven minutes to go, Stamp found Jazz unmarked on the left and he hit a first-time ball into the centre of the field, to where Rory was waiting with his back to goal. The big Dublin-born forward took the ball on his chest with two defenders close at his back, laying it off to Chris just before he was clumped from behind by a clumsy challenge. Chris, running full pelt on to the ball, saw it sit up and beg to be fired at goal.

It was a long way out, but Chris couldn't resist having a dart at it. He arrived over the ball perfectly balanced and let fly. It was rising slowly all the time and bent away slightly at the last minute. The Cathedral keeper tried his best to reach the shot, but the best he could do was a fingertip deflection which touched the ball into the side of the goal rather than the back of the net.

The ball made a sizzling noise as it spun round in the netting, finally coming to rest in the far corner. By then Chris was leaping up, punching the air in delight. It was one of the best goals he'd scored all season and it seemed to have settled the match – not to mention the Championship.

Cathedral, almost bottom in the League, had made a fight of it, even though they had fallen behind in just five minutes to a rare goal from Mac. Now their heads fell in despair. Pulling two back in the last ten minutes would be a desperate task.

Turning back, Chris saw that Rory was taking his time getting up, as if he had been hurt by the challenge. Chris felt a little twinge of alarm, and ran back to join his team mate. Iain Walsh arrived at the same time.

'It's a dead leg,' moaned Rory, in some discomfort.

'OK, no point mucking about,' said Walsh quickly. 'I'll play our other sub.'

Chris's feeling of apprehension grew even wilder. 'Maybe it'll run off,' he said.

Rory looked up at him with daggers in his eyes and Walsh also managed to dismiss the idea without needing to say a word to Chris.

'Stamp's looking really tired. If I bring on a fresh pair of legs now, he can cover for both you. After all, it's only nine or ten minutes to the final whistle.'

Chris looked over towards the bench. They had already used one of the other subs to replace Mac just after half-time. All they had left on the bench were a couple of defenders, a reserve keeper – and Jace. The American was almost invisible at the back of the small group. He wasn't even watching.

'Who will you bring on then? Miller? You know, he could help shore up the back . . .'

Walsh was helping Rory to his feet, letting the big, red-headed forward lean on his shoulder. Rory tested the injured leg and winced as he felt a spasm of pain run up his thigh. Walsh looked at Chris as if he was starting to suspect Chris had sustained an injury as well – to his head.

'We don't need anyone at the back. If we lay off, we'll give Cathedral a chance to dictate the game for the last ten minutes. No, we'll give this cousin of Nicky's a run.'

Chris felt his heart sink.

'Uh –' he began, not sure what he could say. He saw Jazz watching in horror from a few metres away. Walsh continued to move to the touchline.

'Are you sure his registration came through?' Chris called after him, blurting out the question the second it occurred to him. Walsh halted, turning Rory around as well as he looked back at Chris.

'What?'

'Did Sean have time to get his papers in to the League?'

'He wouldn't have suggested that he play as sub if he hadn't!' Walsh snapped in reply. Rory nodded at his side, looking like he was half of a two-headed, three-legged creature.

Chris couldn't think of any other objection he could raise. Maybe it would be OK; maybe they could bluff for ten minutes.

Walsh was still thinking.

'Mind you,' he said at last, 'I haven't had a letter saying it's OK. And if we play Jimmy and his registration hasn't come through, the League might order us to forfeit the match . . .'

Chris glimpsed a distant ray of hope. Walsh continued to ponder the problem for a few seconds longer, with the ref looking at all of them as if they had gone mad. Chris stole another glance to the sideline. Jace was still there, oblivious to what was happening out on the field, his attention fixed in another direction entirely.

Chris turned in the direction Jace was facing and realised why his attention was elsewhere. Sean Priest was walking over towards the game – with Stefan Brodenberg alongside him.

Chris was surprised to see the Dane – he'd hoped that he would be busy with the American team, who were off on a day trip to London. His heart sank. Now that he was faced with the prospect of it happening, he didn't believe for a second that Jace's disguise would fool someone who knew him as well as Stefan did.

He wished they'd had the time (and the idea!) to test the disguise out on someone else first – one of the other Mount Graham players, maybe. Chris didn't feel comfortable about Stefan being first; he had some lingering doubts about Stefan's interest in Jace after that lunchtime meeting in Fair Market. He hadn't dared mention his uncertainty to Priest when he had cooked up this plan. The two men were close buddies – team mates. Priest had even asked Chris if Stefan shouldn't be brought up to date on their little deception. Chris's only excuse for leaving Stefan out of the circle of people in the know was that the fewer people who knew the truth about 'Jimmy', the better.

Priest had seen the sense in that, but he clearly didn't think he had to treat Stefan any differently. And now here he was – the last person Chris (never mind 'Jimmy') needed to see.

His mind was racing. He faced Walsh again, speaking almost before the ideas were formed in his mind.

'Look, there's Sean now. I'll ask him.' He ran off at once, leaving Walsh and the ref having a one-sided discussion about how long it was going to take for Walsh to get Rory off the field so the game could restart.

Chris reached the two ex-Oldcester players as they were rounding the corner flag, still 30 or 40 metres from where Jace was half-hidden among the Colts subs. They were deep in some conversation that Chris didn't manage to hear any of as he ran up.

'Hi!' he called. The two men looked up.

'Hello, Chris,' said Stefan, with his usual friendly grin. Chris nodded back, feeling quite awkward about the deceit he was playing, and fixed his attention on Priest.

'How are we doing?' the youth team manager asked.

'Good,' replied Chris, not sounding too happy. 'We're two-nil up, about ten minutes to play.'

'Looks like we're just in time for the celebrations, then,' Priest said. 'I've been looking forward to this.'

Chris wasn't ready to start celebrating yet.

'Small problem. We need to play a sub and Iain Walsh isn't sure now whether Jimmy Fiorentini is eligible.'

There was a moment when he wondered if Priest was about to ask him who he was talking about, but then his expression went from bewilderment to sudden recognition to stifled amusement in the space of about three seconds and he nodded at Chris as if to say 'I remember!'

'Well, yes, he's eligible . . .' Priest began, watching Chris very carefully. 'I mean, I got him all signed up yesterday. But is Iain sure he wants to play him now? He hasn't even had time to train with the team.'

'Oh yes,' said Chris, more sure he knew what Walsh would want to do than Walsh was himself. 'I think Iain's very impressed with Jimmy. Besides, it's only for ten minutes.'

'OK, if you're sure . . .' Priest said.

I wish I were, Chris thought, as he turned away and sprinted towards the small huddle of players around Walsh and Rory Blackstone. He found Jace hidden among them.

'Get your track suit off,' he said. 'You're on. You'll be playing on the right side of midfield, near me . . .' That would also put him on the far side of the pitch from where Stefan was. Chris noticed Walsh was watching him take charge of the substitution and he shot the coach a weak grin. 'You were right. No problem.' He indicated Sean with a nod of his head. 'Sean says it's OK.'

Now that he'd looked up again, he realised that the two men were still advancing, slowly getting closer. Stefan was busy listening to whatever Priest was telling him, but looking up. Chris almost threw Jace to the floor in his desperate haste to help him remove the track suit leggings. They finally came loose and Chris dragged Jace to his feet and over to the touchline.

He was about to step on to the pitch when the linesman (a father of a boy from Cathedral) stopped them with his arm.

'Hey – what do you think you're doing?' he yelled.

Chris realised the problem at once. The ref had restarted play before the substitution could be made, ignoring the fact that Chris had run off the field as well. Neither 'Jimmy' nor Chris would be allowed on to the field until there was a stoppage. The Colts were down to nine men!

Walsh was still distracted; half of his attention was fixed on Rory, but the rest of his mind was clearly starting to realise that Chris wasn't where he was supposed to be. Chris quickly adjusted where he was standing, so that he shielded Jace from view with his body as best he could. He saw that Stefan and Priest had paused at the end of the group on the touchline, watching Walsh tend to the injured forward. He turned back to face the field, seeing the Colts were falling back as Cathedral tried to take advantage of the confusion.

At that moment, however, Jazz won a tackle just a few metres from them and got away with the ball. He looked up but there was no-one forward of him in a blue and red shirt. He hesitated, looking very confused as he tried to think of something he could do with the possession he had won. When he saw Chris staring at him from the touchline, he looked even more confused!

'What are you doing over there?' Jazz yelled. How was he supposed to pass to Chris while he was standing off the field?

'Put it out of play!' Chris called.

Jazz snapped out of his stupor just in time. The Cathedral full back was tearing towards him like a cheetah after prey. When he was just a metre or two away, and about to launch himself into a fast sliding tackle, Jazz tamely knocked the ball into touch. The defender pulled up, looking cheated. No-one seemed to know what was going on for a moment, but Chris signalled to the ref, who waved him back on.

Chris waited while the linesman checked Jace's boots and then they went on together, running quickly to the far side of the field. He called instructions to the other midfield players as he passed them, reorganising the Colts' line-up.

Cathedral took the throw-in while the Colts were still milling around in bewilderment. They attacked quickly, and it was more poor finishing than good defending that saved the day. Cathedral's striker hit a shot at goal when his partner was unmarked and barely ten metres from goal – Russ dropped to his left and gathered the ball into his chest.

Chris breathed a sigh of relief. With any luck, that would be the end of the drama and they could see out the last few minutes without getting into any more trouble.

In fact, things were about to get even more frantic.

Russ hit a long kick-out, which Stamp headed on. Chris saw the ball was heading straight to Jace.

'To me, Jimmy!' he called. Unfortunately, that broke Jace's concentration (or maybe he just forgot his new name!) and he stumbled as he collected the ball, knocking it back towards the goal.

This time Cathedral made no mistake. The same striker

who had been left frustrated less than a minute before now collected the ball as he ran through at speed, catching the defenders flat-footed with surprise. As he entered the penalty area, he looked up and fired a low shot past Russell's right hand into the back of the net.

The entire Colts team groaned with disappointment. Jace looked at Chris in alarm, knowing it was all his fault. A few members of the Colts team shared the same thought.

'All right, Polly, give up,' snapped Chris as the midfielder offered some ripe comment to Jace. 'He's only just come on!'

'Strewth, Chris – that was such a present for their lot it might just as well have had a ribbon on it!'

'I know, I know. It's not such a big deal, though. We're still a goal up!'

Polly muttered something about how it was unlikely to stay that way for long unless everyone got their act together. Chris clapped his hands and yelled to the nearest of his team mates, psyching them up, then ran over to Jace.

'I'm sorry –' the American began.

'Forget it,' Chris replied quickly. 'Look, let's try to make sure you don't get caught like that again. I want you to man-mark that guy there – the tall lad with the earring. Stick close to him and if he gets the ball, try to tackle him without using your hands . . .'

'Got it,' muttered Jace, but he didn't look too happy.

'You've just got to hang on a few minutes, that's all,' Chris encouraged him. 'Remember, as soon as I take the kick-off, get close to that bloke and stay close. We'll do the rest.'

He left Jace staring at the tall Cathedral midfielder and ran back to the centre circle, where Jazz was waiting with the ball.

'I told you this wouldn't work . . .'

'I don't need this right now!' Chris muttered. He had only told Jazz about the plan because he needed someone who could say they had seen Nicky's cousin play before. Jazz had been utterly unconvincing, but it hadn't mattered. It was Sean Priest's opinion that had convinced Walsh.

Chris stole a glance at the touchline, where Walsh was signalling frantically at the defenders. He could see Sean

Priest's face too, and the coach didn't look happy. He heard the ref blow the whistle for the restart.

'Just try to hold possession as much as you can,' Chris told Jazz. 'Play up to the corners, knock it about. Don't pass the ball to Jace!'

Jazz's face still had that same expression of 'I told you so' on it. Chris glared at him.

'Any chance of you taking the kick-off, Riverside?!' the ref yelled. Chris looked up to find the Cathedral team looking at him impatiently.

Taking a deep breath, he knocked the ball to Jazz, who slipped it back to Stamp. Chris just had time to see that Jace had moved quickly up towards his opposite number and was playing up very close to him. The tall Cathedral midfielder looked quite amazed to find himself tightly man-marked while the other team were in possession.

Not that Riverside held the ball for long. Tosh mis-hit a long pass up towards Chris and Cathedral collected the ball. Their midfield moved it around until they could start their next attack. Chris covered as much ground in midfield as he could and he saw Jazz do the same, starving Cathedral of space. In desperation, the ball was knocked back towards the Cathedral goal and out again towards the left.

The tall lad was trying to shake Jace loose, but this was a game the American could play very easily and there was rarely a centimetre between them. As the ball reached him, the tall guy was forced to knock it back very quickly as Jace closed in from the back.

'Good work . . . Jimmy,' called Chris, almost stumbling over the name. Maybe this might work out yet.

Cathedral switched the ball to the other side and tried again. Tollie was beaten to the outside and a long cross floated right over the box. Once again, the tall boy tried to shake off Jace's attentions and the two raced after the loose ball. The guy from Cathedral just got their first, but Jace was there right after and very enthusiastically.

Too enthusiastically for the ref, who saw Jace bang into the midfielder from the back, sending him sprawling. He blew for the free kick without a moment's hesitation.

Jace gestured at the ref, clearly unaware that he had done

anything wrong. Chris went over quickly before he thought of any words to add.

'Come back here!' he hissed, pulling Jace back by the arm.

'What did I do wrong? He had the ball –'

'Never mind. It's a free kick and you and I are going to form a wall. We just stand still until the kick is taken, OK? Then go back to marking the same guy if you can, but don't touch him!'

'How am I supposed to tackle him?' wailed Jace. Chris wished he and Nicky had managed to get that far in their crash-course on soccer.

'Just get in his way if he gets the ball – don't let him shoot at goal.'

Chris turned so that Russ could position the pair of them where he wanted. The ref made them stand back a bit further (Chris yanked Jace back before his team mate could protest), then whistled for the free kick to be taken.

The tall lad hit a flat, fast cross into the area. Zak headed it out under pressure. One of the Cathedral defenders picked up the clearance and stretched play out to the right with a perfectly weighted pass that put the full back clear on an overlap that left Tollie for dead.

Another cross, aimed at the near post. Chris had run back towards the penalty spot, and arched his head to follow the ball as one of the Cathedral strikers flicked it on. It evaded Russell and the two Colts' defenders with him near the line. It bounced once, and landed at the feet of the tall midfielder with the earring.

Chris's heart leapt into his mouth.

Jace was between the Cathedral player and the goal, a couple of metres off his man. He had lunged for the ball and missed, and was now turning desperately as the other boy got the ball down off his chest, drawing back his foot to fire in his shot.

It would have been a miracle if anyone – even someone who knew what they were doing – could have stopped that strike in the circumstances. Beyond Jace, the goal was almost wide open, with Russell scrambling wildly back from the other post and Zak watching in horror as he saw what was happening.

Jace gave it his best shot. He was big but he was quick. He threw himself forward, arms outstretched, as the midfielder snatched at his chance. Chris watched as the ball flew off the ground and struck Jace an instant later. Jace's head snapped back and he landed heavily, blindly collecting the tall lad as he fell. They tumbled to the ground in a wild display of arms and legs, Jace managing to end up on top.

The Cathedral players – well, ten of them anyway – appealed simultaneously. The only weakness in their argument was that half of them were appealing for handball, the other half for the way Jace had landed on their man like a ballistic missile. Either way, though, they screamed at the ref, who promptly pointed to the spot and blew his whistle.

Chris felt sick. It was almost as if the ref was pointing at Jace and yelling, 'It's his fault!' He quickly took a few rapid strides over towards where Jace had landed.

To his amazement, he was almost trampled in the rush of Colts' players rushing to complain to the referee. Walsh had high standards in that regard, drumming into them that they were supposed to obey the ref's instructions and accept his decisions without question. On this occasion, though, their discipline was forgotten. Zak, the team's captain, led the way.

'Penalty, ref? What for?'

Even the ref, spoiled for choice, didn't seem too sure what to say. In the end he settled for 'handball'.

'Handball? The ball hit him in the face!'

'After it hit his arm,' the ref insisted.

'There you are then!' pleaded Zak. 'He was just protecting himself!'

The referee wasn't about to swallow that. 'Protect himself? He threw himself at that other lad!'

'He was just trying to block the shot!' This was from Tollie. One by one, the other Colts were arriving to join the protest. The ref backed away, continuing to point towards the penalty spot, but they followed him, still arguing furiously.

'It looked more like martial arts to me!' insisted the ref. 'I'm not changing my mind!' That didn't stop the Colts' players from trying and the protests continued louder than ever.

Some distance from the moving argument, Chris had reached the two fallen players. The Cathedral midfielder looked a bit shell-shocked, but otherwise he was fine. Jace's face was marked with a livid red spot where the ball had smacked into his cheek just under his left eye.

'You OK?'

'I think so.' Jace grinned weakly. 'Did I do something wrong?'

Chris didn't answer. Instead, he helped Jace to his feet, then stretched out his arm to assist the Cathedral boy in getting up.

'How about you?' Chris asked.

'I'm fine . . .' the boy squeaked, looking around vaguely. 'What happened?'

Chris left him in the care of the Cathedral coach, who had run round with the magic sponge and a relieved smile. Walsh was on his way too, but Chris didn't think Jace was any the worse for wear.

'Have you ever wondered why they call this football?' he asked, grinning.

Jace touched his cheek gingerly and winced. 'I'm never going to be a big fan of a game called faceball,' he agreed. He looked past Chris to where the Colts' objections were running out of steam in the face of the ref's insistence that his decision stood.

'What happens now?' asked Jace.

'A penalty,' Chris explained.

'Yeah? How many yards?'

Chris decided that Jace could do without a further lesson on the laws of soccer at that point. Besides, he had the impression things were about to get even worse. The ref was advancing on Jace, reaching into his pocket with one hand.

'I'm sorry, son, but that was a deliberate foul in a goal-scoring situation.' He pulled out a red card and brandished it at Jace.

There was a moment of continued pantomime as Jace stood there, unable to comprehend the significance of the gesture, while the Colts' players – now joined by their coach – started a fresh protest.

Chris walked a little closer to Jace and whispered, 'He's sent you off. You have to leave the field.'

Jace turned away slowly and walked off behind the goal-line with Walsh. The Colts continued their angry complaining, milling around the ref until he threatened to book a few of them. Even Jazz was too furious with the official to have time to moan at Chris.

Finally, at the end of three minutes of unhappy confrontation, Riverside's ten remaining players accepted the inevitable and stepped back to watch as Russell took his place on the goal-line and Cathedral's goal-scorer lined up the spot kick.

Russell had a pretty good record with spot kicks – he had saved a couple already this season. In fact, it was something he took a great deal of pride in. Chris tried to cling to the hope that he would show his usual uncanny ability to out-guess the forward, and know which way to dive.

He did. It still wasn't enough.

Russell beat the ground with his fist as the ball went to rest in the back of the net, having missed it by a fraction. The rest of the Colts team lifted their eyes to the bright sky, as if to ask what they had done to deserve such rotten luck.

Chris felt almost sick. He knew it wasn't fate that had brought them this close to losing a game they had been even closer to winning. The Plan was starting to look like it was going to fall apart at its first real test.

Jazz was walking over, his dark eyes cloudy with anger. Chris waited for the inevitable 'told you so' complaint.

'Did you see that?' he yelled. Chris managed a feeble nod. He knew that this was all his fault. He watched the Cathedral players celebrating.

'That was never a penalty!'

Chris looked round. 'What?'

'The ref's stupid. How could he give handball against Jace for that?'

Chris found himself whispering the word 'Jimmy' back.

Jazz recoiled in surprise, then his memory fed his brain and he looked back at Chris with growing comprehension. 'Right, yes . . . Jimmy.'

Chris waited to see if Jazz would say anything different now. All the Asian midfielder could manage was, 'Stupid decision.'

They made their way back to the centre circle. Polly and some of the others were shouting encouragement back and forward between them, trying to find the strength to come back at Cathedral again. No-one mentioned 'Jimmy's' mistake.

Instead, they included him in the general chatter as if he had been in the team for months.

Chris couldn't explain it, but he wasn't about to look a gift horse in the mouth. The whole team was pulling together, determined that their day wouldn't be ruined by a single incident. They were the best and they wanted to prove it.

The Colts tore into Cathedral in the last few minutes of the game, attacking almost non-stop, feverish in their intensity and determination to get back in front. Stamp hit one hopeful volley from twenty metres that the Cathedral goalkeeper saw late and had to scramble back to clear; Jazz was robbed when he had already run through four tackles and a fifth would have left him an open goal; Chris himself shaved the post with a swerving shot after a corner.

When he looked back, past the lonely figure of Russell Jones (who didn't even have to deal with a back pass in that last period of the game), Chris saw Jace standing behind the goal, watching in bitter disappointment. Even from a distance, he could see how miserable the American was. He exchanged a few words with Russell and Chris saw the keeper – who had had his own problems when he first signed up for the Colts – smile and offer him some crumb of comfort that had made Jace laugh.

Others in the team looked back at different times too and they all gave 'Jimmy' the thumbs-up. Seeing him behind the goal instead of on the field made them even more determined.

All their efforts were frustrated though. The final whistle blew on the 2–2 draw. The exhausted Cathedral team gave their opponents three rousing cheers with the last breath they had and then half of them fell to the floor.

Zak led the reply, which was understandably half-hearted in the circumstances. The Colts trooped off to be greeted by Walsh in one of his more forgiving moods.

'Good try, lads. That was just bad luck at the end there.' He didn't mention the two goals they had let in, but Chris saw the coach look across the group at him and he recognised the warning he received.

'What are the other scores like?' asked Jazz, who had remembered that it was still possible for the Colts to win the Championship after a draw, provided that two other results went their way (including Nicky's team, Gainsbury Town, winning at home).

Walsh looked at his watch. 'Give them a few more minutes. Sean said he'd call someone at the two grounds.'

'Where is Sean?' asked Zak, looking around.

'Talking to your new player,' replied a heavily accented voice, and while the others turned to look towards the goalmouth behind which 'Jimmy' had been standing, Chris turned to face Stefan.

Their eyes met. Had he been fooled, Chris asked himself, wondering how he would ever be able to tell for sure.

'A rough debut,' the Dane continued in a subdued voice. There was a long pause. 'I remember my first game for Brondby. I got sent off too.'

Chris nodded, too dumbstruck to speak. It *had* worked. Stefan believed in 'Jimmy', the new player in his first game for the Colts.

'Tell Sean I will meet him back at the car, OK?' Stefan smiled. He pulled his coat a little tighter, pushed his hands into his pockets and walked away. Chris was almost sorry to see him go.

No-one else even noticed. They drank the isotonic juice Walsh handed out and munched through some fruit, all of them watching as Priest finished his conversation with 'Jimmy' and the two of them started to walk slowly back towards the touchline. Sean had dipped into his pocket and pulled out his mobile. No-one spoke as they waited to hear if their luck had been any better on other pitches than it had been on this one.

The first call was over by the time the two of them reached the huddle. Jace took the drink offered by Walsh and went to sit by Chris and Jazz. Chris grinned at him and he was glad to see that Jace smiled back.

'That was my Uncle Fabian,' the American replied, hiding his accent as best he could under a rather comic Italian one. He'd clearly been rehearsing that opening line as he'd walked back. 'Gainsbury won two-nil. Nicky got them both.'

The Colts cheered loudly. That result was good enough to put one of their rivals out of the title hunt. Walsh told them to hush. Priest had finished dialling and was speaking to someone at the other game.

'Mike? Hi, it's Sean. How're you doing?' He listened carefully to the answer, avoiding making eye contact with any of the Colts team. It must have been an ordinary conversation, because it was Priest who steered the call towards the important business at hand. 'We drew two-two, so we really need to know how you guys got on.'

Another pause. The silence around the small huddle of Colts' players, with a few parents and others around them, was so complete they could almost hear the answer the tiny voice on the mobile gave them.

Priest, still listening, shook his head. At once, that small hope they had shared evaporated. A few heads fell. Chris felt Jace start to get up alongside him, but quickly reached out with his hand to pull the American back down.

Priest was wrapping up the call. He switched the phone off and slid it back into his pocket.

'They drew two-two as well. That means they're on thirty-five points with two to play; you're on forty-one. They can get level on points, but they have to score three goals more than you on the way if they're going to take the title. That's assuming, of course, that you sad acts can't find a point from either of your last two games.'

His face opened into a genuinely warm smile. 'Maybe it's better this way. The next game is at home in two weeks' time. Win that and we'll have a slap-up Sunday feed at my house to celebrate. Come on, cheer up. It's still going to be your year!'

That lifted a few spirits, as did the fact that Walsh chose to highlight all the things they had got right rather than dwell on the way the game had been allowed to slip away. In fact, the closest he got to a complaint was when he pointed out that they should have put five goals past Cathedral in the first half alone, in which case it wouldn't have mattered what happened in the last ten minutes.

Slowly, they started to drift away towards patient parents on taxi duty. Chris and 'Jimmy' were being picked up by Polly's father and they were just on their way back to his comfortable Espace when Sean Priest called them back. Nearly everyone else had gone and Iain Walsh was occupied with stowing kit in the back of his car. They could speak privately.

Chris thought he knew what this was going to be about.

'Look, I'm sorry about today –' he began.

'What for?' asked Priest, genuinely surprised.

Chris flicked a glance at Jace and tried to think of a way to handle this delicately. 'You know . . .' he began, lamely. 'We tried to do too much, bringing Jace into the Colts like that . . .'

'Don't blame Jace for what happened today,' Priest insisted, frowning as he spoke. 'Iain was right; the game should have been dead and buried, even at two-nil. You guys relaxed too early and Cathedral were still in the game. What happened with Jace was just – well – dumb luck.'

Chris was thrown more than a little off-balance by this statement and he stumbled over a succession of 'buts' and 'errrs' without stringing together anything that made any sense.

'Besides, I agreed to go along with this crazy scheme of yours, even though I can't begin to understand it.' He looked from Chris to Jace and back again. 'Look, I know that Jace has some problem – Benford told me that the day you arrived, when he explained why you were here instead of Stockton . . .'

And now he was posing as someone else, in a different team, thought Chris.

'He didn't tell me what the problem was – just that you had had to leave your parents and that he couldn't just leave you behind when he came over here.'

Priest waited patiently to see if Jace would supply any additional details. Chris, who had done his fair share of waiting in similar circumstances, was completely unsurprised when Jace said nothing.

'I said it was none of my business then and I guess it still isn't now, even though you have managed to involve Chris, Nicky, me and who knows who else in this strange game you're playing. I still can't believe I'm going along with this "Nicky's cousin" business. But you can't go on like this, Jace. Sooner or later, you've got to resolve whatever this problem is, so you can get your life back to normal.' Priest ran his hand through his hair. 'My life too.' He shifted his attention to Chris, a playful smile on his face. 'You know, when I became youth team manager at Oldcester, I thought my life would revolve around teaching kids to play good football . . . training, matches, the odd injury scare . . . How come, Chris, that ever since I've known you, I've been caught up in one strange adventure after another? Fights, arguments, disappearances . . . not to mention a fire and a kidnapping.'

When he heard it put like that, Chris had to admit it had been a pretty busy year since he had first met Priest.

Chris was all in favour of things getting back to normal, but the conversation wasn't really aimed at him, so he stood quietly to the side and waited for Jace to show some sign that he agreed. Jace, however, just listened quietly as Priest told him how things couldn't go on like this for ever, saying nothing. Chris wondered if it would help if they could offer some kind of answer to Jace's problems, but he also knew that they didn't have a clue what to say.

Priest must have reached the same conclusions. 'OK, Jace,' he said. 'We'll leave things as they are for now. At least I know you're safe and well while you're at Nicky's. But I won't help you run away for ever.'

That seemed to be that. Chris was already turning away as he heard Jace mumble some thanks to Priest and they were both trudging steadily across to where their lift was waiting when they heard Priest's mobile warble.

Something told Chris that the call would involve them and he turned back just in time to see Priest's face light up with surprise. He waved at Chris to go back, speaking softly into the phone as he did so. The two boys returned to see Priest was struggling to hear the call properly; he had a finger in one ear and a pained expression on his face as if he was pressing too hard.

His eyes settled on Jace. He looked grave.

'Jace,' he said. 'It's your father.'

Ten

For the second time in just a few days, Chris found himself in Oldcester city centre, walking through Fair Market. There were no crowds around this time, though – it was Sunday afternoon. Now that the pubs were closed as well, Fair Market was almost deserted.

A few families were taking advantage of the warm sunshine to stroll through the narrow streets, window shopping or killing time until the next showing started at the Odeon on St James's Street. Chris examined every face he saw closely, trying to see if anyone he recognised was watching them.

Jace was doing the same thing, his face tight with tension. He had the earphones of Chris's Walkman plugged in, his baseball cap jammed on top with the peak to the back and his hands thrust deep into the pockets of his jacket. It didn't make him look any more relaxed.

The last member of their little trio was Sean Priest, who was equally alert, but who didn't have the same chalky pallor and grim-faced expression the boys were wearing. Every now and again he checked the two boys at his side, as if he was worried that they might not be there for long. Walking in a row like that reminded Chris of some dodgy old Western, with the good gunfighters walking down the centre of the street, straight as an arrow, towards the ambush the guys in the black hats had set. Chris found himself looking up at the skyline for the skinny guy with the rifle who was always the first to get shot (allowing the stuntman to fall off the roof in a slow, rolling arc).

He didn't share this thought with Jace or Sean Priest. He doubted that either of them would appreciate it just at the moment.

As they approached The Wanderers, Priest slowed their pace, as if he wanted to have more time to check out the lie of the land ahead. Jace glanced up at him, then fixed his gaze firmly forward into the circle of iron girders and pillars.

Chris was looking in the same direction now. He could see the man who had come to the house sitting at one of the tables. He looked up and saw them as they emerged from the narrow street. He stood up, smiled and waved.

Jace didn't look quite as delighted to see him. Chris had a moment to wonder if it really was his father, but – almost as if he'd guessed that the others might have doubts – Jace whispered: 'It's him.'

The three of them stopped to take a long look around their surroundings. There was no-one else in sight who didn't look as if they belonged: just families; an old man with his dog; a few lads of about seventeen loitering by one of the shop doorways and yelling loud 'jokes' at each other; a man and a woman holding an edgy, unhappy conversation on the steps around the fountain. Chris watched the lads for a moment, feeling threatened by their loud presence. In the end, he convinced himself that there was nothing more suspicious about them than their complete lack of a sense of humour and some well-dodgy haircuts. There was no sign of Ripley, Mr Pony-tail or anyone else who looked like a CIA agent, a member of the Mafia or a mad axe murderer.

So far, so good. It looked like the 'other side' were sticking to their agreement.

They stepped into The Wanderers, walking over towards where Mr Goodman was standing, looking just as nervous as they felt. Chris took another moment to look around at the other occupants of the circular space. It still looked all right. He crossed his fingers and hoped that they weren't about to make a big mistake.

⚽

That first call had been a brief one.

As soon as the caller had rung off, Priest had told them the gist of what had been said.

'He said his name was Robert Goodman. He sounded American, quite a soft voice . . .'

Jace had nodded, although it didn't prove much.

'What did he want?' asked Chris.

'He says he wants to talk to Jace.'

That news wasn't very surprising, but Chris had found himself intrigued by the way it had arrived. Why call Sean? Why a phone call at all; why not just turn up?

While Chris had considered these 'clues', Priest was giving Jace the rest of the information. 'He said he'd been told I knew how to get in touch with you. He says he just wants to talk; he knows you're frightened, but that you don't have to worry. We can meet him anywhere we want. He said he'd come alone.' Priest had looked at Jace, to see how he took all this unexpected news. 'What do you think?' he asked.

'We don't even know that it was his dad!' Chris protested.

The caller had thought of that. 'He said that he bought you a computer for Xmas. He said he hoped you were looking after it like he told you and knew what to do with it.'

Jace nodded. Chris's memory had convinced him to speak up. 'You said he bought you the camera for Christmas. The computer was the year before . . .'

'No, it's OK,' Jace insisted. 'It's him.'

Chris had thought about starting one of those protests that could only begin with 'But you said . . .', but had thought better of it. Jace had decided that he wanted to make the meeting with his father.

'He'll call back in an hour, to find out where and when,' said Priest.

The three of them had stood there looking a little foolish for a moment, as if they had to wait there until the phone rang.

Chris had looked around St Paul's Fields, wondering if the caller was in sight somewhere, having watched them and seen through Jace's disguise. It wasn't a comforting thought. He almost wished he hadn't mentioned it to the others.

'Chris, will you stop behaving as if this was some kind of Tom Clancy novel?' said Sean. Chris had no idea who he was talking about; they'd never studied anyone called Clancy at school, but from the sound of it he'd be a better bet than Dickens or any World War One poet. 'He didn't ask to speak to Jace, he just said he believed I could get in touch with him.'

'So how did he get your number?' asked Chris.

'I don't know!' Sean exploded, clearly in no mood to play whodunnit. Chris had already decided that it had to be Stefan Brodenberg, more from instinct than any particular reading of the facts.

'Someone must have told Jace's father we knew where he was.'

'I know,' said Priest, clearly troubled by that fact himself. 'But they don't know about this little masquerade you're running. If they knew that 'Jimmy' was really Jace and that I was here watching him, wouldn't they have asked to speak to him directly?'

That had made sense, if little else had. Chris hadn't liked the feeling that they were being followed all the time. Now, perhaps, it seemed they weren't. The Plan was still working, and Mr Goodman's sinister shadow, Jackson, couldn't just reach out to grab them . . .

'So, Jace?' Priest asked. 'What do you want to do?'

'We need to talk . . .' Jace said, sounding as if he was both dreading and looking forward to the prospect at the same time.

After a few more minutes, they had realised that they didn't have to wait around like lemons on a stall. They had let the boys' lift go and had walked off St Paul's Field in the direction of Priest's car.

As they had rounded the corner, Chris saw Stefan Brodenberg leaning on the wing, reading a newspaper. Priest groaned at the same moment – they had forgotten that Stefan was with him.

'I'm going to have to tell him something . . .' said Priest. They had all ducked back round the corner.

'You can't!' cried Chris. He was still gripped by a feeling that Stefan was involved in the mess somehow and it didn't help when he noticed a telephone box on the corner, outside the newsagents. Had Stefan used it to call Mr Goodman? Perhaps buying a newspaper so he'd have change?

'So what do you expect me to do?' hissed Priest.

Chris had no idea. He just knew that it would be madness to have Stefan with them while they went to see Jace's dad; not to mention the fact that Jace was still in his 'Jimmy' disguise. Although it had passed inspection from twenty metres away, Chris didn't think it would fool Stefan within the confines of Priest's BMW.

'I'll have a word with him,' said Priest, and he disappeared around the corner. Chris and Jace had remained where they were, not even daring to take another peek. When Priest had reappeared, they almost jumped out of their skins.

'It's OK, he's gone,' he said, beckoning them to follow him round the corner. 'He's got to go and see one of the other Americans – Bennington, the guy staying with Tollie.' Tollie lived in a rambling old house that had once been a doctor's surgery. Luckily, it was close enough to walk.

The three of them had piled quickly into Sean's car and he drove away through the light Sunday traffic. There was only one place to go first – back to Nicky's house, so that Jimmy could wash the colourant out of his hair and off his skin, as well as lose the corset. By the time he had reappeared as Jace, Chris had eaten a huge 'snack' provided by Mrs Fiorentini.

More importantly, Sean had already taken the second call and fixed up the meeting in The Wanderers.

Mr Goodman looked as trashed that Sunday as he had earlier in the week when he had arrived at Chris's place. His hair was uncombed and he had some very un-designer stubble on his chin. There were dark rings around his eyes and his skin was pale. He looked as if he hadn't slept for a week. Although this might have been because he was deeply worried about his son, Chris doubted it.

This was the first time Chris had seen Jace together with his father and he wasn't sure how they would behave. From what he had seen on *Baywatch*, Californian fathers and sons gave each other big bear hugs, slapping each other on the back as if they were both choking on something.

Goodman father and son, on the other hand, stopped some small distance apart, both looking nervous and ill at ease meeting up like this. Mr Goodman hesitated like he was going to offer to shake Jace's hand or something, then he pulled a chair back from the table at which he had been sitting, and gestured for Jace to sit down.

He turned his attention to Sean briefly as Jace took his seat.

'Thank you for agreeing to meet,' he said, offering his hand to Sean.

'Don't mention it,' Priest replied in a low voice.

Mr Goodman offered Chris a weak smile that showed he recognised him, then sat down. Chris wasn't sure where he was supposed to put himself, but he finally settled for following Priest's lead and taking a place at the neighbouring table, close enough to lend support, but far enough away to allow the Goodmans to talk without being overheard. Not unless Chris really concentrated.

'How're you doing?' Mr Goodman asked, awkwardly.

Jace shrugged a non-committal reply, then broke the silence that followed by observing, 'You look awful.'

They exchanged a few other catch-up pleasantries after that, which made Chris wish he wasn't trying so hard to hear every word. It was like one of those times he had visited his aunt in Sheffield; there wasn't really anything they could say to each other, but they had to manage something just to fill up the silence. Jace and his father were really struggling to get past the awkwardness of the situation and on to the meat of the matter.

'You want a Coke or anything?' asked Sean, abruptly (perhaps he had been listening too). Chris hadn't seen anywhere open, but he said 'yes'. Priest managed to interrupt the thrilling conversation at the other table long enough to find out that one of the coffee shops was open and that Jace would like a Coke too.

The break actually did some good. As soon as Priest had walked away, Mr Goodman leaned back in his chair and said, 'We really have to talk, Jace.' Chris knew that meant he really shouldn't listen, which meant that he turned away so that they could have a little more privacy – and listened even harder.

'Go ahead . . .' Jace said sullenly.

His father took a little time to compose himself before he tried to get the ball rolling. 'I'm glad you're all right. I was really worried something would happen after you left San Francisco that night.'

'Something did happen!' snapped Jace angrily. 'Marion's thugs followed us and tried to force us off the road.'

Chris jumped a little when he heard that name. Although

he had the strange sensation of knowing that he'd never heard it spoken before, it was hauntingly familiar at the same time. He spoke the word a few times in his mind to be sure. Marion, Marion, Marion . . . The sound didn't jog his memory at all.

He had a pen in his pocket and jotted the name down on a napkin on the table. M-A-R-I-O-N still didn't jump out at him. He was left, though, with the strange feeling that it should have done . . .

The conversation had moved on while he was preoccupied, but Chris hadn't missed too much. Jace was still recounting how the 'goons' had chased his mother's Cherokee along the Pacific Highway.

'Then we lost them – there was nearly an accident and they must have been stuck behind it. Mom pulled off the road near Big Sur at that beach we stopped at last summer – you remember? We hid in the forest and waited for you, just like you said. Then a car came and it gave the signal you told us to wait for . . .'

Jace paused then, as if he was gathering himself for the next part of the story. Chris almost turned round, but he managed to steel himself, and fixed his gaze on the couple by the fountain, who seemed to be very tense with each other despite their holding hands routine. You think you've got problems, Chris thought.

Jace's voice sounded hard and brittle as he continued.

'Only it wasn't you, it was Marion and his goons. Mom got out of the car – I heard shots. Two of them chased me down to the beach, but I managed to lose them. By the time I got back to the car park, Marion was talking to some cop and then they all drove away. I couldn't see what had happened to Mom, but they found the Cherokee and drove it away.'

Chris knew the broad outline of what had happened from there. Jace had walked back up to the highway during the night and hitched a ride to LA. From there, he had called his uncle in Newark, who had sent him money and an air ticket. And from there he had come to Oldcester.

Jace's voice was shaking now, as if he was close to tears.

'Do you know what's happened to Mom?' he asked.

'She's OK. I don't think Marion would hurt her.'

'I heard shots!'

Mr Goodman offered a thin laugh. 'More than likely your mother. I can't imagine she would let herself get taken easily.'

'They were talking about getting rid of her . . .' Jace insisted. That seemed to destroy what little confidence Mr Goodman had.

'He says she's OK . . . we have to believe that, Jace.'

'Believe Marion? After what he's put us through? How do you know Mom's all right? What if . . .?'

Neither of them dared take that part of the conversation any further, frightened of where it might lead. Mr Goodman's voice was sounding full of emotion, as if he was extremely fearful of what might have happened. Jace was exploding in acid anger.

'This is all your fault!' he yelled. Chris saw the couple look up, distracted from their own intense conversation by the ruckus at the tables. Chris grinned in embarrassment and tried to look as if he wasn't really anything to do with it.

At that point, Priest reappeared and the growing storm calmed down as he delivered Cokes and cappuccino coffee. He sat down at the far end of Chris's table, further away from the Goodmans, but facing them. Chris looked at him and read the concern in his face.

The argument, softened slightly after the interruption, began again. Chris could have been sitting at a table on the other side of The Wanderers and he would have heard every word. Priest was blocking his view of the couple now, but he bet they were listening intently.

'Look, Jace – I made a mistake, sure. But how was I to know Marion would still be interested in me after all these years? And how was I to know he'd come after your mother and you?'

'You know what he's like! That's why we had to run away the first time. As soon as he found you, he was always going to come looking for us. You made it easy for him!'

'Jace . . .' Mr Goodman's voice was full of defeat. In contrast, with every word he spoke, Jace sounded shriller and harsher.

'Did you tell him Mom and I were driving back to LA that night? Did you tell him where we were supposed to meet you? He even knew the *signal*! You must have sold us out!'

'Jace, I swear, it wasn't like that!'

It didn't sound like Jace was interested in finding out what it was like. He had worked up a real head of steam now and was tearing into his father without restraint. Chris tried to imagine what it could be that was making Jace so angry with his father; he couldn't imagine ever speaking to his own dad like that. He couldn't even imagine being that angry with his mother and he knew how much he resented her leaving home.

Jace's problem went a lot deeper than just seeing his parents split up, that was clear. Mr Carter had said how close Jace had stayed to his father. They didn't sound that close any more. In fact, Jace sounded as if he would happily have killed his father at that moment.

And Mr Goodman sounded like he would have let him.

'Listen to me, Jace. I don't have time to argue with you about this now. You've every right to be angry, but you're wrong about me. I would never have put your mother in danger. You have to believe that.'

'Yeah, right,' said Jace.

'I'm sure your mom is fine, but we both know that Marion's using her to get us to do what he says. You understand that, don't you, Jace? If we don't do what Marion says . . .'

Chris felt icy fingers down his spine. This was starting to sound more and more serious. He could see Priest's jaw had tightened too, as if he was becoming just as uncomfortable with what he could hear.

'No, Dad!' Jace yelled. Chris heard his chair scrape along the floor, as if he was leaping to his feet.

'Listen, Jace!' Mr Goodman cried desperately. 'You have to come back with me! We have to give Marion what he wants! Then he'll let us go!'

'That's a lie! As soon as he has all of us, he doesn't have to worry any more. He can do what he likes!'

Chris felt Jace bump into his chair from behind. Priest was getting to his feet, clearly worried that Jace might be about to pull one of his disappearing stunts. Chris could no longer fight the temptation to look round.

Jace was backing away, his eyes full of tears. His face was bright with rage and his fists were clenched low at his side. Mr

Goodman was half out of his seat too, his hands stretched out, pleading with Jace to wait.

'Jace, I'm begging you . . . we have to do what Marion says.'

'No!'

'Yes! What choice do we have? You can't stay here in England for ever – and every second you do, you risk getting even more people involved!'

Priest was now alongside Jace, putting his hands on his shoulders. Chris imagined he was starting to say that he thought it might be best if they called a halt to the meeting there.

As he watched him open his mouth to speak, Chris realised they were not alone. The couple from the fountain were moving towards Priest; the man very close, the woman reaching to move a chair that blocked her from getting to Jace. Chris froze; everything happened at blinding speed.

There was a sickening, dull thud as the man struck Priest hard over the back of the head. In the same instant, as Jace screamed and Mr Goodman yelled 'No!', Chris jumped forward instinctively, lashing out with his foot.

He was about to get very involved indeed.

Eleven

Chris's foot made solid contact with one of the white metal chairs, sending it tumbling and clattering over the paving stones towards the woman as she made a grab for Jace. It smacked into her shins, skittling her over. Human and metal legs became entangled and her shrill shriek of pain got caught up with the ugly rattle as the chair hit the floor. Her grasping hand just missed Jace's sleeve.

Chris was more accurate. He reached out and tugged at Jace's arm.

'Come on!' he roared.

He had a moment to observe the four adults as he yanked Jace back, before he turned round to follow the American in a headlong dash across the floor of The Wanderers. Priest was sinking to the ground, his eyes folded tight with pain and shock, his legs buckling; the woman's eyes were closed as well as she felt the pavement rise up to crack against her arm and hip. Jace's father was horror-struck, his mouth gaping wide as he realised what was happening around him.

The man was the only one to look in control. He had a small cloth tube in his hand, which hung heavily from his fist. As Chris watched, he let it go and it fell to the floor with a soft thud, like wet sand falling on hard rock. The man's eyes were a crystal blue, brilliantly intense, and were focused on Chris with raw hatred for his interference. He had a broad skull, wide eyes and dark hair shaved close like Julian Dicks. Thinking about it, Chris realised he was even less keen to meet this guy down a dark alley than he was the West Ham full back.

There was a narrow, tight-lipped grimace on the man's face and his hands looked brutishly powerful. Even as he turned away, Chris saw the man lift one of the tables and flick it aside, instantly clearing a path for his pursuit.

'Run!!!' he yelled at Jace, in case his team mate had managed to forget in the last few micro-seconds.

Jace was sprinting off ahead of him, looking to find a clear path through the tangle of identical furniture haphazardly scattered across the central part of The Wanderers. Chris followed, jumping and hurdling, twisting and turning. With almost every step, he yanked at the back of a chair, trying to pull it across behind him to block their path. The air filled with the raucous clatter of the furniture as Chris scattered it in their wake and 'Julian' slammed it aside.

Thanks to the furniture, the boys were just about pulling ahead. Chris could feel the gap growing. As they reached the edge of the cafe area, he risked a look back. They'd put about ten metres between themselves and the man; his companion was back on her feet, racing around the perimeter, still quite a way off. There was no sign of Mr Goodman.

Not that Chris was that worried about him at that point. Ahead, Jace was hesitating as he emerged from the jumbled central area into the wide paved circle in front of the shops. There seemed to be a lot of people looking at them, but no-one was exactly jumping in to help. Chris wondered about calling for help, but instinctively he knew that this wouldn't be Jace's first choice.

He flew past Jace, taking control of the direction of their flight, even though he didn't have a much better idea of where they were headed. The boys stretched their legs, following the steady curve of the pavement, heading towards the nearest of the small roads that led away from The Wanderers. Their pursuer was still too close for Chris to feel they could shake him off, even in the narrow streets of Fair Market, but what else could they do?

They had one other advantage, though. Although he clearly possessed a lot of brute strength, the man wasn't exactly Linford Christie on his toes. The gap was actually holding. In fact, as they thundered past some bewildered Sunday strollers, stretching their legs still further, the boys were actually pulling away.

'This way!' called Chris, spinning round another corner.

He could hear Jace behind him, and the heavier thump of the man's boots as he turned the corner. At the next corner, Chris took a glimpse over his shoulder and saw how close he was – his eyes glinting, his teeth fixed tight.

They were heading up towards St James's Street. Chris wondered if the man would dare attack them in the middle of the busiest street in Oldcester and decided it would make little difference to him; he had pursued them through Fair Market in full view of everyone. So, how were they going to lose him?

He didn't have time to think of an answer. As they turned again, into a shop-lined street that was narrower than some alleyways, Chris collided with someone carrying cake boxes from the back of a bakery towards his car. It was a colossal hit, like something in a cartoon, with boxes and cakes flying off in all directions as Chris slammed into him.

They hit the ground simultaneously. Chris felt a sharp ringing in his ears and realised he had caught his head on the baker's elbow. Through the white noise, he heard Jace shout. It sounded as if he was miles away, or trapped in a deep canyon. The voice echoed for a moment and then was gone.

Or, rather, it was replaced by the anguished howl of the baker, who was surveying the way his wares were displayed in a ring all around where they lay. Chris picked himself up as far as his hands and knees and instantly felt sick. He was covered in icing, cream and marzipan and the sweet scents clogged his mouth, making it hard to breathe. Fighting the nausea, he tried to pull himself up to his feet.

The baker wasn't keen to see him go. Chris felt the guy grab hold of his arm.

'Oh no you don't, you young idiot! Have you seen what you've done?'

Chris didn't need reminding. There was no sign of Jace or the sinister blue-eyed man anywhere (it dawned on him that this wasn't what the baker was concerned about). He looked both ways along the street, but it was empty of dangerous kidnappers, at least as far as he could make out. The dark alley opposite seemed to be the only option.

The baker could sense that Chris was about to run off and leave him amidst the ruin of his craft. He tightened his grip.

'Are you listening to me? I said who's going to pay for this lot?'

Chris tugged, not expecting to be able to break free, and he and the baker were equally amazed when Chris's arm slipped easily out of the man's greasy hands. Chris's jacket was liberally smeared with cream, which made him as slippery as an eel swimming in Vaseline. The baker tried to get up, but his shoes slithered through the same gooey mess.

Chris wrenched himself clear and staggered into the street. He was about to plunge into the alley, when he took one more look back the way he had come. No Jace, no 'Julian', but he did catch a glimpse of the rapidly retreating figure of a woman. *The* woman.

Still feeling fuzzy-headed, Chris lumbered off after her, almost spilling to the ground at the first step. He felt very dizzy. It took a huge effort just to stand and here he was trying to sprint.

She moved quickly, but she was even less Sally Gunnell than her mate was Linford, so Chris managed to keep her in sight. There was the added complication that she kept looking round, obviously trying to see which way 'Julian' had gone. Chris hugged the side of the street (which had the added advantage of allowing him to stumble against a wall whenever the dizziness got too much). Somehow she didn't see him.

She wasn't just searching blindly – she was definitely heading in a solid direction. It took Chris a while to work it out and he only managed it then because she actually dashed through the door to the underground car park while he was watching.

Of course! They'd have to have a car! 'Julian' could hardly carry Jace under his arm through the streets of Oldcester. It had been risky enough snatching him – now they would want to make a swift getaway. Chris knew he only had a few seconds to stop them. He felt the nausea lessen its hold on him a little and summoned up his reserves of strength and will to continue the chase.

He reached the door to the car park twenty seconds after she had. Beyond, a tight spiral staircase wound down around a lift shaft. The lift's car was below them somewhere and the woman hadn't waited. Chris could hear her short-heeled boots clattering down the steps, echoing off the cold, tiled walls.

He took a step towards the stairs. At once the nausea returned at full power. As he watched, the curving stairway seemed to writhe and twist, until he couldn't tell up from down. He felt himself tumble and grabbed for the handrail. The clattering boots were suddenly a very long way away.

He forced himself to wait, breathing deeply. The world returned to normal (or as normal as it could be when you're chasing someone who has abducted an American who may or may not be related to some kind of master criminal . . .). Trying hard to get a grip on himself, Chris stumbled down the stairs.

There was a distant bang and the clattering ceased. Chris froze for a moment, but he knew the woman was no longer on the stairwell.

'Damn!' cried Chris, knowing she must have reached the deck on which their car was parked. He ran past the next couple of landings, Blue and Red (colour-coded to help drivers remember where they had left their vehicles), trying to judge how far ahead she might have been and which deck she might have gone on to. In his heart he knew that – even if he guessed right – each deck could hold 150 cars and he might never spot them until they roared up the ramp away from him.

Finally he plumped for Green.

He swung back the door. Ahead, the vast concrete floor was almost completely empty.

Of course! It was Sunday! With the shops closed, there weren't so many cars in town. Chris felt a glimmer of hope. There might still be time.

He scanned the area around him. There were only a dozen cars on Green deck, and none of them were occupied. Nor could he see anyone moving around. He turned back, slammed through the door and descended to Orange.

He was acutely aware of just how much time had passed – there was no point trying to be clever or quiet. He crashed through the door on to Orange deck, hearing the sound echo like thunder around the vast, almost-empty space. Three faces whirled round in his direction.

'Chris!' yelled Jace loudly.

The man and woman were pressing him down, trying to force him on to the rear seat of a black Vauxhall Vectra. The woman's face was alarmed, surprised at being interrupted. The man's face was impassive, but Chris knew that he wasn't welcome.

'Get the kid in the car,' 'Julian' snarled at his partner, leaving her with Jace squirming frantically in her arms. He started to walk purposefully towards the stairwell, teeth bared in a dog-like grin. The car was twenty or thirty metres away, but he was closing the distance fast.

Chris stepped back, then turned quickly and ran round the bare concrete wall that surrounded the stairwell. He heard 'Julian' curse, and the heavy fall of his feet echoing around him.

Running round and round the stairwell didn't seem like much of a plan for getting Jace rescued, but it was all he had for now.

As he passed around the back wall, he noticed a fire bucket hanging from a hook on the wall. There was nothing else in view that seemed to offer any possibilities, so Chris took a moment to check if there was anything inside. There was – sand, along with a few cigarette butts and other litter.

'Right!' came a savage cry.

Chris looked up in alarm – the man had tricked him, doubling back to run round the stairwell in the opposite direction (now, why hadn't Chris thought of that possibility?). He was reaching out towards Chris, his face tight with anger and spite.

Chris moved with instinctive speed, dipping his hand into the cold sand in the bucket and picking up a fistful of loose debris. He flung it at the man's face.

'AHHH!!'

The effect was better than he'd hoped for. With his hands outstretched, 'Julian' had no way of protecting his face and the loose sand and ash hit him in the eyes with stinging force. He staggered, yelling loudly.

Chris dodged around him, running at full speed towards the car. The woman was wearing the same amazed expression she had been wearing earlier. She wouldn't have had a clear view of Chris's actions from where she was standing – all she would have seen was her partner staggering back as if he had been taken out by Steven Seagal.

She didn't look as if she was prepared to argue as Chris raced towards her. Jace slipped her grip and sprinted away from the car.

There was another stairwell at the far end of the deck. Chris altered course towards it, shouting at Jace to follow. He didn't dare take a look back until they reached the door. 'Julian' was rubbing his eyes, supported by the woman, who was pointing in their direction as she led her companion towards the car.

'This isn't over yet,' said Jace, although he gave Chris a short grin that suggested he wouldn't be sorry to be proved wrong.

They fled up the stairs three at a time. By the time they reached the street they were gasping for air. Chris was pretty sure he had heard the sound of tyres squealing on the ramps the cars used to reach ground level, but he didn't panic. Fair Market was pedestrianised – cars weren't allowed in. The exits from the car park all opened on to the two main roads on either side.

'Which way now?' puffed Jace.

'I think we should find Sean . . .' Chris panted in reply. He took stock of his bearings, then started to lead the way back towards The Wanderers.

'Wait!' called Jace. Chris turned and saw that Jace was burrowing in his jacket pocket. 'Take this.'

Chris held out his hand and Jace dropped the small plastic film container into his palm.

'What's this all about?'

'If they get me, I don't want them to get this too,' replied Jace quickly.

'I think we're safe now . . .' Chris started to say, but he stopped when he saw Jace shake his head.

'You were right before. Sooner or later they're going to catch up with me. I have to stop running and start thinking about how I'm going to get out of this mess once and for all.'

Chris closed his fist around the film container and thrust it into the pocket of his jeans. He wanted to ask Jace what was on the film, but he held the question inside. Jace wasn't ready to open up even though he was asking Chris to go further and further out on a limb. Maybe he was involved in something really dodgy, but Chris couldn't say no to his American team mate.

'You can trust me . . .' he said.

After another moment, they started along one of the narrow streets towards the centre of Fair Market, keeping a wary lookout behind them in case 'Julian' didn't obey traffic regulations.

There were no familiar faces in The Wanderers as the boys arrived. Jace's father and the Oldcester coach had disappeared. After a second look round, Chris decided that there were some familiar faces, but they belonged to the young men who had been loitering around earlier. They were still in the same place, drinking from cans and bottles and telling each other rude jokes.

It was quite nice to see them again.

'What now?' Jace asked, suddenly very full of questions.

'First we find a call box and ring Sean's mobile; let him know we're OK. Then we go back into hiding.'

Jace groaned. Chris wondered if he preferred being chased by thugs and kidnappers to pretending to be Jimmy Fiorentini.

'If you don't like the idea, come up with something new yourself. But don't expect anything else from me. I don't know what's going on, remember?'

Jace looked him square in the eye for a moment and Chris could see something had changed in the way Jace was thinking.

'OK . . . I'll tell you everything . . .' he said.

At last. Just what Chris had been waiting for.

That was when he heard the roar of the car engine.

⚽

The woman was at the wheel. She had been forced to creep along the narrow back streets of Fair Market, but as soon as she reached the wide pavement around The Wanderers, she revved the engine and spun the car's wheels as she sped towards where Chris and Jace stood.

One of the vehicle entrances to Fair Market must have

been open, Chris thought. Some of the shops took deliveries on Sundays and the woman had known about it. That meant she was local. Hired help.

The thought that he was up against common criminals and not some CIA mastermind came as some slight relief to Chris as he stood there, watching the car racing closer. It took him several long seconds to get his brain working on the more immediate problem.

'Run!' he yelled, and he and Jace took off together. In different directions.

Chris had spotted the flaw in the woman's approach, which was that she couldn't chase them through the dense, tumbled seating of The Wanderers. She'd have to stop the car and get out if she wanted to catch them. If they could keep her at bay long enough, surely someone would come to their aid or call the police.

Jace, however, had opted for direct flight. Before Chris realised he was gone, the American was haring off towards the nearest side street, which just happened to be the one near where the youths were standing.

Chris skidded to a halt a few metres inside the circle of tables and chairs. The car flashed past him, its brakes squealing as the woman stood hard on the pedal. She'd overshot the turning.

Chris heard the gears crunch as she tried to get the Vectra into reverse. Clearly, Jace was her target – she wasn't going to come after small-fry like Chris. Thinking quickly, he grabbed a chair and threw it out on to the road behind the car. Without seeing where it landed, he picked up another and sent that in the same direction, then another. He kicked a table over too. This was starting to become a habit.

The space behind the car filled quickly with crashing, bouncing metalwork. The woman was looking out of the side window, glaring at him. He saw her start to open the door.

The guys in the doorway were watching all this as if it was great entertainment. They jeered and howled with laughter as the car door caught on one of the chairs and the woman struggled to get it open. One of them leaned forward and banged on the car's bonnet.

'Want a hand, darlin'?' he bawled.

The woman's expression didn't suggest that she would appreciate his help. In fact, she looked quite murderous. The car's engine revved again and she drove back about ten metres, crashing through the tangled barricade Chris had thrown in her path. One of the chairs caught under the rear bumper and there was an angry shriek of metal. She halted the car at once.

The youths thought this was hilarious and crowded closer.

She wasn't going anywhere, at least not in a hurry. One-nil to the good guys, Chris thought to himself. Judging by the boisterous mood the young men were in, they would keep the woman entertained for long enough for both Chris and Jace to escape.

His triumph lasted for all of five seconds. The woman opened the door wider and stepped out, her eyes fixed on Chris's. Then she turned to face the youths who were now clustered in front of her car. In a single fluid motion, she dipped into her pocket and pulled out something that gleamed dully.

Chris didn't have a clear view from where he was standing, but the youths did and they seemed mightily impressed. They backed away from the car, their faces wide with surprise and fear.

The woman started to turn.

Chris didn't need a closer view to confirm that she had to be holding a gun. One-one, thanks to a late substitution. The game had just become a lot more exciting.

Chris's instincts were still operating at lightning speed. There was a gap of about twenty metres between himself and the driver's door, and plenty of furniture. He fell to the floor.

It wasn't, he thought later, that he thought she might shoot him. That kind of thing just didn't happen on quiet Sundays in sleepy English cities, did it? No, he just figured that it made sense to not allow her to threaten him in some way that might allow her to catch him. That was it.

Chris crawled away from the spot where he had landed as quickly as he could. She might not be able to see him, but his own view of the situation was just as restricted.

After a space of about 30 seconds, he heard a voice shouting a woman's name. There had been some other noise in the meantime – a few shocked screams and shouts from around The Wanderers – but this voice sounded as if it belonged.

Chris took a peek over the top of a table and his heart sank.

'Julian' was moving quickly towards the car from the side street Jace had fled down and he had the struggling American in his grip. The woman was already ducking back inside the car, leaning over the seats to open the passenger-side rear door.

At this distance, there was nothing Chris could do. 'Julian' more or less threw Jace into the car and climbed in after him. There was a brief moment of stillness as the woman looked across the cafe area to see if Chris was close enough to grab as well, but then he heard the muffled shout of the man telling her to go. The car's wheels burned rubber as she floored the accelerator and fish-tailed the car across the pavement, then it turned into the same street as 'Julian' and Jace had appeared from and disappeared.

One-two. The home crowd had gone very quiet.

Twelve

Monday. Chris stayed in bed late, although he hadn't been able to sleep much. All night, he had replayed the events of the previous day through his head like a favourite video. The action sequences were as clear as day, even if he didn't understand the plot.

He checked his watch. Half-past nine. He could hear his father downstairs talking to someone and it didn't sound like an altogether friendly chat.

His father hadn't been in a very good mood last night either. It was probably something to do with the police arriving to tell him that his house guest was the suspected victim of a kidnapping. After the events of the previous autumn, the subject of kidnapping was a bit of a sore wound in the Stephens' household.

Chris had given the visiting detectives the edited highlights of what he had been part of in Fair Market. There had been plenty of witnesses to the abduction, so there was no point denying that something had happened. Chris was still working on the assumption that Jace wouldn't want the police involved, however, so he had tried to make it sound a lot less dangerous than it had seemed at the time. The fact that this also made it sound a lot less dangerous to his father was an undeniable bonus.

The detective left without knowing much more than he'd arrived with, promising to return the next day.

Which meant that all Chris had to do for the rest of the day was deal with his father's questions, which weren't so easily avoided.

He hadn't been able to dodge them all night, though. Mr Stephens knew his son too well to accept half-answers and silence. Chris knew that there would be more of the same today.

Perhaps if he stayed in bed . . .

'Chris! Get down here!'

Oh well . . . Chris swung his feet out of bed and got dressed. His father was waiting impatiently at the foot of the stairs. His face was as black as thunder.

'I hope you've had some time to think about all this,' he snapped by way of greeting. 'I want some answers this morning, young man.'

Chris paused on the stairs. His father walked off into the kitchen.

Chris drew a deep breath and followed him in. He wasn't sure if the presence of Sean Priest drinking tea was a surprise or not.

The two men exchanged a distant, cold stare, then both turned to face Chris as he slipped quietly through the doorway. Mr Stephens took up position in front of the sink, leaning back as he waited for someone to speak.

'Something has been going on behind my back. Something to do with Jace. I want to know everything.'

Chris felt the same way, although he decided that it wouldn't be wise to admit this out loud right now.

'OK, no more games,' said Priest. He looked at Chris. 'It's gone too far already, Chris. The police are involved, whether Jace wants them to be or not.'

Chris kept silent.

'Start with what happened yesterday afternoon,' said Mr Stephens.

Priest opened the account, although – of course – he couldn't tell Chris's father too much anyway. One minute there was a conversation between Jace and his father and the next Priest's lights had been turned out.

'I didn't even know Jace's father was in the country,' Mr Stephens commented, sounding very bitter. He would be even less impressed, Chris thought, if he discovered how much more he didn't know.

'I'm not sure Jace did until a day or so ago. As far as I know, yesterday was the first time they'd seen each other since Jace came to the country.'

Chris's father looked at him for confirmation. Chris nodded. He was very glad no-one asked if anyone else had met Jace's father before . . .

'So, you set up this meeting. That means you knew how to find Jace. The last anyone told me, he was staying at someone else's house. No-one said he'd run away.'

Chris remembered that his father hadn't heard about the 'Jimmy Fiorentini' scam before today. He had been going to tell him, but things had moved too fast. Even though he'd been told that things were under control, he must still have been very worried about what might have happened to his house guest. Chris felt very guilty for what he'd put his father through.

Priest must have been feeling the same way. The story skipped on.

'Jace's mother and father split up some time ago. Jace told me he still saw his father and that they had been getting on OK . . . When Jace said he was prepared to meet his father, I agreed to go along.'

Mr Stephens moved his attention to his son. 'And you tagged along as well?' he asked. Chris nodded. 'So what happened next?'

'This man and woman knocked out Sean and grabbed Jace . . .' Chris said. It seemed safest not to provide any details.

'The police said something about a gun –'

'I never saw one,' said Chris, which was stretching the truth more than a little. He doubted that the dull, metallic object in the woman's hand could have been anything else, judging by the reaction of the youths in front of her car.

Mr Stephens considered this information for a moment and decided not to pursue the details of the event.

He turned back to Priest.

'I can't believe you've allowed yourself to get involved in all this,' he said flatly. 'You're supposed to be looking out for the kids in your care, not getting them involved in kidnapping.'

Chris thought that was a little unfair. Priest didn't actually have any responsibility for him and he couldn't have known what Jace's father was planning. On the other hand, he had participated in the various deceptions that had been going on since Jace stepped off the plane. He decided to let Priest fight his own battles.

'Looking back, I'd be happier if things had gone differently,' Priest admitted. 'When the Americans first arrived in this country, Benford Carter told me Jace was his nephew and that there was a family problem that was best solved by Jace leaving the States for a while.'

'Is that what he called it?' asked Mr Stephens. 'A family problem?'

Priest nodded. 'It didn't make any difference to me or Oldcester United or the Colts who they brought, so I said fine. Benford said Jace had travelled over on his passport, pretending to be Stockton. He said he was using the name Carter, but that it would be too difficult for Jace to remember to answer to the name Stockton all the time, so he was going to be Jace Carter while he was here. He was hoping to throw anyone who might come looking for Jace.'

'Turns out he was right – someone did come looking for him.'

If only the phony name had worked, thought Chris.

His father was considering what he had heard. If that had been all there was, there would have been no real problem – it was a small white lie, that was all. Jace Carter, Jace Goodman – what was the difference?

'OK, I can understand that,' said Mr Stephens at last. 'I would have preferred to know the truth, but I can live with it.' He turned to Chris. 'When did you find out?'

'A few days after he arrived,' Chris confessed.

His father looked disappointed. 'OK,' he said, returning his attention to Priest. 'Why did he run away?'

Priest shot a glance at Chris. 'Someone came looking for him.'

'His father?'

'Among others . . .' said Priest.

'And they were going to try and grab Jace – to take him back to America?'

'That's what we thought,' said Priest. 'So when Chris found him, we thought it would be best if he stayed at Nicky's for a while. And we cooked up the "Jimmy Fiorentini" disguise.'

'That sounds like one of your half-baked ideas,' said Chris's father. Chris grinned back weakly. Mr Stephens focused on Priest again, considering everything he'd been told. 'If you were so worried that Jace was in danger of being abducted, why didn't you go to the police?'

Chris sighed, trying to disguise it by turning away to get a can of Virgin cola from the fridge.

'Jace wanted to avoid the police,' replied Priest. 'He said his father would be in real trouble if the police were involved. We all needed time to think. I don't think any of us expected things to come to a head so quickly.'

'I see . . .' said Chris's father, although it was clear he knew that he didn't and that the others were keeping some of the details from him. 'And now Jace's father has abducted him anyway . . .'

Chris took a small sip from the cup. That was the problem. After all they'd been through, Jace had been grabbed anyway.

'No,' said Priest. 'It wasn't his father.'

Chris almost choked on the cola. This was news to him!

'What do you mean?' he said, his voice high with surprise.

'It wasn't Jace's father who arranged yesterday,' Priest insisted.

Chris was speechless. If it wasn't Mr Goodman, then who?

'How do you know that for sure?' asked Mr Stephens.

Priest drew a long breath. 'Because after the couple went chasing off after Jace, Mr Goodman helped me recover my wits. Then we went looking for Jace together. I was with him all night. He was in my house when the police called to ask me about Jace's abduction.'

Mr Stephens looked more confused than ever. Chris wasn't sure he understood anything any more either.

'So . . . if this isn't about Jace's father snatching his son back, what is it?'

Priest took a deep breath and stood up.

'Ask him yourself. He's outside in my car.'

⚽

'You know quite a lot of it already,' said Bob Goodman. Chris almost laughed out loud. He was starting to wonder if he knew anything at all.

'I don't!' his father protested. 'Just start from the beginning, OK?'

Robert Goodman sighed, his face even more lined with

worry. He was sitting on the living room couch, just as he had on his last call. He appeared to have borrowed some of Priest's clothes since then, but he still looked haggard and tired. Chris was sitting on the floor beside the armchair in which his father was perched, leaning forward with his elbows on his knees.

The atmosphere in the room was very strained. Everyone was waiting to see what the Jace Goodman affair was really all about.

'It started a long time ago, when Jace was little. I was asked to do a job for this guy – some renovations on a hotel in upstate New York. I'm an architect, you see.'

That was a lot less interesting than Chris had expected. He could only imagine what Nicky would make of it.

'I went up there, took all the measurements and drew up the plans. Only, while I was working I discovered that parts of the place weren't safe. The contractors had used sub-standard materials – the place was a death trap, a real fire hazard. I told the owners, but they weren't interested. So I warned them that I'd have to tell the authorities.'

Chris's mind was racing ahead, trying to imagine Ripley as some kind of buildings inspector. It didn't seem likely. Perhaps this was going to be a longer story than he imagined.

'They got real nasty,' Mr Goodman was continuing. 'They warned me to keep my mouth shut or they'd cause me real trouble. I thought it was just threats. I spoke to some guy I knew in the sheriff's office, and he contacted the FBI. Next thing I know, I was being arrested.'

'What for?' asked Chris, almost caught out by the sudden twist in the story. His father reached down and tapped him on the back of the head, trying to encourage him to keep quiet.

'Someone planted some stuff in my car. It's very complicated, but the short story is that the hotel was owned by some guys who had some connections with organised crime. They had some bent cops working for them; guys on the take. So, when I started causing trouble, they broke into my car.'

'What was this . . . stuff . . . they planted?' asked Mr Stephens.

Mr Goodman looked very embarrassed. He looked up once at Chris's father's totally innocent face, then avoided any eye contact with anyone as he replied: 'You know . . . stuff . . .'

Chris remembered the names the other boys had called Jace in the dressing room. He figured he knew what the 'stuff' was and knew that his father wouldn't be able to work it out from any subtle hint. At the same time, Mr Goodman didn't look comfortable talking about it. Chris decided to move the story along and bring his dad up to speed later.

'So what happened next?' he asked.

Mr Goodman looked relieved, offering Chris a small smile. He took a sip from the mug of coffee he had been given. Chris noticed that his hands were trembling. His voice sounded raw and emotional as he continued the story. 'The guys who owned the hotel offered me a deal . . . they'd make sure the charges were dropped and the evidence got "lost" if I withdrew my allegations about the hotel and kept quiet about what I knew.'

'And did you?' asked Mr Stephens.

Mr Goodman's shoulders dropped. Chris guessed at once that Jace's father hadn't been able to avoid giving in. Something told him that it must have been a pretty rough decision. He knew how Jace would have felt when he found out about it. Any kid would have wanted the story to have continued with his father standing up to the mob and being a hero. Jace's father had taken a different course. Jace loved his father, but Chris knew that the truth about him hurt.

'I had a young family. I did what I was told.'

There was a brief silence while everyone took this in. Sean Priest ended the pause.

'How long ago was all this, Bob?'

'Ages ago . . . ten years, maybe. Jace was only little.'

Chris took a long drink from his can of cola and waited for the tale to continue. Mr Goodman sat back in the sofa and stared off into space. 'That was the end of it for a little while,' he said, 'but then this guy started coming to the house asking me to do some work for him. I said no, but the guy insisted. He said that if I didn't agree to help, he'd bring all that old stuff out into the open again and have me sent to prison.' He carried on quickly as if this was the hardest part of the story. 'So I did some work for them. Nothing much. They just wanted an architect's name on the plans they'd already drawn up. I wouldn't do anything more than that.'

He looked around the room quickly, as if seeking their understanding. Clearly, things were about to start getting serious.

'Anyway, a year later there was a fire at a property they owned in Carolina. Nothing I'd been involved in, but I knew it would be the same kind of place. A girl got killed. That was when I decided I had to get out. I went to another FBI office in another state and told them the story. I gave them all kinds of evidence. They said they had enough to put Marion away for good.'

That name again! This time, Chris knew at once where he had heard it before. It was part of the e-mail address on the message Jace had received. He could guess where this was all leading.

'Even so, it was going to take a year to bring the thing to court, so they put all of us into the Witness Protection Programme. We left New Jersey, went out to California. A year later, I went to court and testified, and Marion got five years.'

Chris could almost picture the scene in the courtroom. 'And Marion swore he'd get you for what you'd done . . .' he murmured.

To his surprise, Mr Goodman smiled. 'Actually, no. He went down quiet as a lamb. No threats, nothing.'

Chris was almost disappointed.

'So . . . what happened after that?' asked Chris's father, equally caught out by the way the story was turning out.

'Nothing, for almost seven years. Marion did his time, came out . . . and still nothing happened. The FBI figured he was concentrating on some new ventures and would just forget about us. They gradually stopped keeping an eye on us. And I thought, hey, maybe it really is all over. I'd been working as an illustrator with a greetings card company all that time and I was ready to get back to doing some proper work.

'So, I set up in practice again. We were using new names . . . and we hadn't been in contact with our families for almost ten years. I figured, who was going to come looking for us now?'

'Marion,' whispered Chris, and this time he was right.

'You got it . . .' replied Mr Goodman. 'He may not be a big wheel, but he has good contacts. He's Armenian, or something. There are small communities all over the States. Anyway, within three months he'd found me again. He threatened to cause me some real trouble. I knew how much this would hurt Grace and Jace –' Chris winced. He hadn't put the two names together like that before.

'What could I do?' Mr Goodman asked, but clearly not expecting an answer. 'I had to agree. I tried to keep it from Grace, but she found out. She said that if we were going to go through all that nightmare again, we might as well give up the false identities. Marion said "no". I didn't fight it, so Grace left me.

'That was the final straw. I decided I had to get Marion off my back for good. So I started collecting evidence again. He was doing all the same kind of stuff as before. Picking up building contracts, doing the work on the cheap and getting me to say everything was up to standard. I tried to keep copies of all the plans, but Marion was wise to that.

'Then, a few weeks ago, I got lucky. I was alone in my office for just a few minutes with a camera I had bought for Jace. I managed to take some pictures of some paperwork that would prove Marion was up to his old tricks again. I contacted Grace. She was bringing Jace up for a visit from LA – that was where she'd been living for the last few months. I told her we could get Marion sent down again.

'I gave her the camera with the film in it. I told her to tell anyone who asked that it was Jace's, a Christmas present. Then I arranged to meet her at this place down the coast.'

'Why didn't you leave San Francisco with her?'

'I wanted to contact the FBI, get the ball rolling again. So I stayed behind in San Francisco while they set off. Only I got caught. A secret security video in my office saw me take the pictures, give the camera back to Jace, and arrange to meet Grace on the coast highway. Marion saw the recording an hour later and locked me up while he went off after my family. He caught Grace, but Jace got away.'

Chris knew the next part of the story well enough. In his mind, he skipped over Jace getting across-country to his uncle's place in New Jersey, and Benford agreeing that the best thing to do would be for Jace to go to England in Stockton's place. He could hear Mr Goodman explaining that part of the story for his father's benefit, but he was piecing together the remaining parts of the puzzle in his head. At last, he figured he had it all.

Except for one thing.

'How did Marion know Jace was in England?' he blurted out. Everyone looked at him. The story had only just caught up to that point.

'I'm not a hundred per cent sure . . .' said Mr Goodman. 'I always figured that he worked out that Jace didn't have that many options and guessed he would make contact with his uncle. When he heard Benford was in the UK, he must have guessed that's where Jace would be.'

Possible, thought Chris, but not that likely. Chris had his own theory about that part of the tale, but for now he kept it to himself.

'The rest you know, I guess . . .' Mr Goodman concluded. 'Marion brought me with him to help persuade Jace to be sensible. When it didn't work, he must have hired some people to grab him.' His whole body shook as if he was sobbing inside. 'So, that's it. He has my wife and now he has Jace – everything he came for. There's nothing left I can do.'

The two other adults nodded their heads sympathetically. It really did look as if all the bases were covered.

'But Marion didn't come all this way looking for Jace!' Chris exclaimed. Everyone turned to look at him. He went from one face to another, amazed that they couldn't see it. 'He had your wife hostage already. That was enough to get you to do what he wanted. It wasn't Jace he came to find, it was the camera!'

Mr Goodman nodded, the only one not energised by Chris's outburst. 'That may be true, but Marion told me he had already recovered the camera –'

'The camera, yes – but not the film!' Chris cried.

Even Mr Goodman looked suitably amazed by that.

'Jace took the film from the camera? But he wouldn't have let it out of his sight . . . not unless –'

Chris stood up and walked to the small chest of drawers beside the fireplace. He opened the top drawer and felt around inside for a small envelope. He turned round and opened his fist like a conjuror. The film canister sat in his palm.

'Not unless he was in real trouble,' said Chris.

Thirteen

Chris was more nervous and excited than he could remember. He could feel his heart beating as he dressed and his hands seemed incapable of fastening buttons. It took him almost 30 minutes to get ready.

His father was downstairs waiting, staring into the mirror and fidgeting with the lapel of his suit jacket. Chris lifted the collar of his shirt a little higher and the jacket finally lay the way it was meant to.

'Thanks,' said Mr Stephens in a low voice. 'Are you about ready at last?'

Chris almost couldn't answer. He wasn't sure if he was ready for tonight or not. All he knew for certain was that it was too late to back out now.

'I'm really not happy about this . . .' his father said.

They stood in the hall, looking at each other for several seconds. Finally, Chris felt some of his confidence returning.

'It'll be all right. There won't be any trouble.'

Mr Stephens wasn't convinced. 'You shouldn't be involved in all this,' he said sternly.

Chris sat on the stairs and pulled on his shoes. He managed to get the laces tied at the second attempt. 'I am involved,' he said. 'I have to be.' He stood up. He was ready to go. 'Besides,' he said, with an encouraging smile. 'You'll be there as well. I can't get into any trouble this time.'

⚽

Priest had phoned early on Tuesday morning. Though his father took the call, Chris had been able to hear most of what was said.

'They've made contact.' Sean's voice, distorted by the

speaker, had sounded extremely agitated.

Mr Stephens had raised an eyebrow and taken a deep breath.

'What did they say?'

'Just like we figured. The film for Jace and his mother. They're going to deliver Jace to the dinner at Star Park tomorrow. I told them that was the only location we would agree to.'

'What about Jace's mother?'

'They'll let her go after the swap. Marion says he'll call the States the moment he has the film. His people will put her on a flight back to New Jersey.'

Mr Stephens had nodded his head thoughtfully. 'Is Bob happy with this?'

Chris heard the pause before Priest answered. 'Not exactly. But what choice do we have?'

'It's not too late to call the police . . .' Mr Stephens had said. Chris had rolled his eyes in dismay. After all they had said the previous day . . .

'We can't, John,' Priest had replied, his voice sounding calmer now. 'As long as Marion's people have Grace, we can't pull any stunts.'

'We're not equipped for this, Sean. If Marion is that bad –'

Priest had cut him short. 'Bob Goodman says Marion isn't a killer or anything like that. It'll be all right. I wouldn't have let it get this far if I thought any of us were in real danger.'

There was a long pause while Mr Stephens digested that opinion, but finally he had agreed to let things go the way Bob Goodman wanted. He had put down the receiver and looked hard at Chris.

'You heard that? Good. Now, let's get one thing straight. This is nothing to do with us any more. We aren't involved. If I had my way, we wouldn't even go to this stupid dinner. But I suppose we have to. But there's just one rule you have to obey – keep away from the swap.'

Chris had opened his mouth to protest, but his father had held up his hand to silence him before the first word could be said.

'You've got to promise me, Chris! Just let Mr Goodman hand over the film and get Jace back. Do you understand?'

Chris had nodded.

'OK,' his father had said, 'I'm off to work. I expect to see you here after practice today.'

'I'll be here,' Chris had said, after he uncrossed his fingers. Maybe he was too old to believe that counted for anything, but he was desperate . . .

Football grounds are strange places away from match days. A place built for twenty or thirty thousand people to worship their idols – cheering, singing and joking – seems more than just a void when the fans aren't there. Some people said it was like an empty church, but Chris had always felt that a football stadium was different. Even empty, a church is still a church. Without spectators, a football ground is just a rectangle of bare stands around a green park.

It was even more noticeable at night. There were no floodlights blazing above Star Park as they drove up to the gates; no queues at the turnstiles. It was quite tranquil.

Chris found himself looking around for Marion or anyone suspicious as his father drove into the car park. He pulled himself up, trying to remind himself that he was being paranoid. This was going to be a simple swap and he wasn't even going to be involved.

After all, he'd promised, right?

He felt a twinge of annoyance that his father had placed such a restriction on him (overnight, the crossed fingers thing had started to seem a little ridiculous). He was sure his presence at the swap would be helpful. Just how, exactly, he wasn't sure, but he knew Jace's prospects would be greatly improved if he was there.

After all, he knew what Marion looked like. Or, at least, he thought he did.

Marion had to be Jackson, didn't he? Chris had convinced himself that the sinister stranger who had called at the house with Mr Goodman that first time could only be the crooked Mr Marion. It annoyed him intensely that he hadn't been able to check it out with Mr Goodman (if he'd brought it up, it would have told his father that Jace's father had been to the house before . . . that was one of the details he'd felt more comfortable in leaving out of the version of events he had told his father). It annoyed him even more that he hadn't known about Marion before. If he'd known, he could have warned Jace that his father was being accompanied by their worst enemy.

They would have been ready for Marion's ambush in Fair Market.

Knowing that made Chris even more determined to be there for Jace tonight. Maybe that crossed fingers thing was going to have to work after all.

Mr Stephens parked the car. There were plenty of others there before them – they weren't exactly late, but they had cut things a little fine. Chris waited while his father locked the car door and then they made their way to the entrance to the Easter Road Stand. Once again, Chris was struck by the stillness of the evening and how strange it felt to be at Star Park when there wasn't a game on.

The evening had been arranged long ago, when the exchange with Mount Graham School had first been agreed. Although Oldcester United hadn't been able to work directly with the Americans, they had made their training facilities available and done as much to make the trip a success as they could. Tonight's gathering was a special dinner held in the visitors' honour. United had arranged for it to be held in the executive dining room at the club.

Chris had been there once before, as part of the thank you the club had arranged for him and Nicky after they had found Sean Priest's collection of memorabilia last year. The idea of another posh celebration at Star Park would normally have thrilled him, but his attention was elsewhere. All he could think about was the swap that was due to take place later.

He took another look around the open space outside the stand as they waited for the main door to be opened. There was nothing unusual to be seen.

Once inside, they climbed up to the area where the club's directors had their special boxes overlooking the pitch, turning along a plush, carpeted hall to the dining room. Much as it had been the last time he was there, the room was brightly lit, with rows of tables set along the length of the room. Many of the other guests were already there, and the room was buzzing with chatter. The Mount

Graham squad were scattered all over the room.

Chris saw Sean Priest right away, talking with a man he didn't recognise. Several of Oldcester's players were there too, sitting at different tables, talking to the guests. There were other young men at the tables too. Chris thought he recognised a couple of them.

A waiter in a crisp white shirt and a smart waistcoat pointed out their table. Chris followed his father across the room.

As he passed between the tables, he could feel eyes watching him closely. He looked to one side. Lowell, one of the Americans Chris had sparred with in the changing rooms at the practice ground, was staring up at him, his face hard and his eyes steady. From the top table, alongside United's beaming chairman, Mason Williams was watching him too, looking every bit as grim.

'Hey, Chris!' came a voice.

They had reached their table. Chris dragged his eyes away from the hostile glare of the Americans to find that he had been seated at the same table as Russell Jones. It was good to see a friendly face.

'Hey, Russell. Did we miss the soup?'

Russell grinned back, waiting for Chris to take his place.

'We've done well here,' he whispered, leaning across the table to share a conspirator's whisper. with Chris. 'Two empty spaces; all the more food for us.'

Chris glared at Russell, who could be incredibly dense at times. One of the spaces was the one that would have been reserved for Russell's father. Unsurprisingly, Mr Jones hadn't honoured the evening with his presence. From the little Chris knew of him, he wouldn't have wanted to have missed some gripping game show on ITV. The Jones household had just acquired a second-hand TV – overnight they had all become candidates to appear on *Telly Addicts*.

The other obvious space, though, was where Chris's partner was supposed to sit. Chris stretched over and turned the name card round for Russell to read. Jones blushed and started to stammer out a 'I didn't mean it' apology as he realised what he'd said.

'Don't worry about it. Jace will be here. Just a little late, that's all.'

As he said this, he looked across at the American sitting just along from Russell, a guy named Toby Something-or-other. Although he was staying elsewhere (for obvious reasons, he couldn't stay at the condemned pit the Jones family called home), he had been paired off with Russell on the exchange. He looked as happy as the other Americans.

Wonderful, thought Chris. He switched his attention round the table to see who else was sitting with them. It appeared that there was a United player on every table, along with another guest.

Chris recognised Oldcester's full back, Les Coventry, easily enough. Even if Chris hadn't been a regular at Star Park, he would have seen Les's face on the local TV news and in the papers over the last few weeks – Blackburn, Everton and Chelsea were all after him amidst rumours that he might get called into the England squad.

The other guest was familiar too, although it took Chris just that bit longer to place him. He knew the guy was a footballer the first second he saw him, but it took a while longer to place him. Steve Potts, the West Ham defender.

Potts stretched out his hand, smiling as he leaned across the table to say hello, and catching Chris off-guard. Had he spoken his thoughts out loud?

'My name's Chris Stephens,' he replied. 'This is my dad.'

The two men shook hands and muttered polite but embarrassed greetings to each other. After a while, Chris started to believe that he hadn't actually blurted it out when he'd recognised Potts. Perhaps he could have another go at the introductions.

'It's Steve Potts,' he told his father. 'Plays for West Ham.'

'I know,' Mr Stephens whispered.

Despite feeling like hiding under the table, Chris took a long look round the room. He was able to name one of the other men he thought he'd recognised – Kasey Keller of Millwall.

Chris groped for the connection. Players from other clubs weren't that unusual as visitors, but these weren't the normal faces. Suddenly, the link popped into Chris's mind.

'You're all Americans,' he said, turning back to face Potts (he ignored Toby, who was sneering at him in a 'Have you only just worked that out?' sort of way). 'All the guests are American.'

Potts grinned back at him. 'That was clever! I don't think too many people would have worked that out. There are a few of my team mates at West Ham who probably couldn't tell you I was born in the States.'

'I collect Merlin stickers each year . . . it says where everyone was born in the book you stick them in.'

Potts was buttering a bread roll, still smiling. 'I didn't think it was my accent. My friend from New Jersey here didn't even figure me for an American until I told him.' Toby looked away quickly before Chris could gloat. 'Your youth team manager thought it would be a neat idea if your guests could see just how many of us are playing over here,' Potts continued. 'Give them some encouragement.'

'Who else is here?' asked Chris, looking round.

'I didn't get to meet everyone. Three of us came up from West Ham – me, John Harkes and Ian Feuer. We gave Kasey a lift from Millwall. I saw Jurgen Sommer from Luton and Brad Friedel earlier –'

'That's three goalkeepers!' laughed Chris.

'Yeah,' said Potts, grinning. 'I don't think you'd put together a very balanced team from the guys who are here.'

The last of the guests arrived while the group on Chris's table chatted about the differences between football in the USA and the UK. Oldcester's chairman, Dennis Likely, a huge man with a dark, bushy beard, made an introductory speech and then the first course was served. Everyone seemed to have relaxed. It woke Chris up with a start when he realised that he had forgotten about Jace completely.

Before the main course was served, Sean Priest walked over to their table. Chris's father looked at him warily, as if he was suspicious that Priest was about to rope Chris into some hare-brained scheme connected to the Jace trade.

'How are you doing?' Priest asked.

'OK,' replied Chris. 'I don't see Mr Goodman.'

Priest shot him a warning glare to remind him that the swap was supposed to be a secret, but Chris had chosen his words carefully and Priest clearly realised this after a moment.

'He's waiting downstairs . . .' he replied slowly. He looked around at the rest of the table. 'His . . . delivery . . . isn't due until after we've finished dinner.'

Chris nodded in the direction of the top table. 'Where's Mr Carter?'

Priest looked back over his shoulder as if he was reminding himself that the American wasn't there.

'Talking to the police, I think . . . about Jace . . .'

Everyone looked suitably serious at this point. They all realised that it should be difficult to celebrate when one of their team mates had been abducted (that part of the story was no secret; it had even been in the paper, but no-one outside of Chris, his father and Priest was supposed to know about Mr Goodman meeting Marion's thugs to get Jace back).

Chris could see Stefan Brodenberg talking with Mr Likely, reliving old memories of when he was a United player.

'So . . .'

'So we just sit tight and wait for news,' said Priest. He gave Mr Stephens a quick look that said he knew he'd promised to keep Chris out of trouble, then left to circulate round some of the other tables.

Chris stood up.

'Chris –' his father began.

'I just need the loo,' Chris replied.

'Just remember what we agreed,' said Mr Stephens, as if Chris had any chance of forgetting.

He left the dining room and made his way to the toilets along the hall. His business there took about 30 seconds. He was on his way back when he realised he was going past the door leading to the stairs.

He only intended to take a peek. He was genuinely going to keep his promise and not get involved.

When he looked out of the window overlooking the car park, however, he saw a car flash its lights twice and a tall, stiff figure step out of the shadows below.

Mr Goodman walked slowly in the direction of the car. He stared straight ahead. Perhaps he could see the occupants of the car. Chris couldn't, but he knew who they were and he knew that it meant that they had started the proceedings early.

He took the first flight of stairs three at a time.

Fourteen

'That will do, Bob,' said the man by the car door. He was leaning on the roof, one foot on the door sill. His grey hair was ruffled slightly by a strong, chill evening wind. His floor-length coat was buttoned tight and he was wearing gloves. Compared to the dishevelled and tense Mr Goodman, he looked completely at ease. Of course, compared to Mr Goodman, a guy facing a firing squad would have looked more calm and relaxed.

Jace's father stopped abruptly about ten metres from the silver Mercedes. He stood in the open driving space between two rows of cars, completely exposed. The suit Priest had lent him fitted him about as snugly as a tent.

Marion looked him over as if he was worried that he wasn't eating right.

'You look a mess, Bob,' he said, with friendly familiarity.

'I'm grateful for your concern,' Mr Goodman replied. 'If we get this over with, perhaps I'll start feeling a little better.'

Marion spread his hands in a gesture of acceptance. 'Fine. No point wasting time, is there?'

'Apparently not. I thought this wasn't meant to happen for another hour.'

Marion grinned. 'I like surprises, don't you? I thought you'd appreciate having more time with your son and less time thinking about any little tricks.'

Mr Goodman didn't reply. Both men heard a distant booming noise and turned round to look at the huge black shadow of the stadium. Marion's eyes narrowed as if he was expecting to see policemen appear from all sides.

'You haven't prepared any tricks, have you, Bob?'

'Of course not!'

'No police?'

'I told you . . . nothing! I'm not stupid, Marion!'

Marion grinned, his teeth gleaming like a fox's. 'The jury's still out on that, Bob. Your lovely wife seems to think you've been real dumb.'

Mr Goodman gritted his teeth and took his time before he replied. 'I was stupid to have allowed you to find us again. I won't allow that to happen again.'

'No, I suppose I'll have to accept that our little business partnership is over,' agreed Marion. He pouted. 'Pity.'

'Just let it go, Marion. I swear, there are no police and no tricks.'

Marion took a deep breath and seemed to grow taller as he straightened up. 'You know, Bob?' he said. 'I believe you. I think you're basically an honest man.'

In an instant, the false jollity on his face vanished. His eyes gleamed like distant points of light in the darkness.

'You have the film?'

Mr Goodman reached into his pocket. 'Here,' Mr Goodman replied, as he drew out the canister.

Marion squinted, trying to get a clear view.

'You know, something just struck me, Bob,' he said flatly. 'How do I know you haven't had the film developed? How do I know you don't have prints and negatives stashed away somewhere?'

'No!' cried Mr Goodman. 'I haven't – I wouldn't . . .'

He looked close to tears. The desperation in his voice was as sharp as a ripsaw blade. Marion was grinning again – a crafty, ugly smile without any humour in it.

'You know, I believe that too.' He removed his foot from the sill and took a pace back to the rear door of the Mercedes. He jerked it open and reached inside. Jace tumbled out into the open.

Mr Goodman staggered half a step forward in a mixture of relief and concern. Jace looked all right and even managed a small smile when he saw his father. Marion kept a close hold on Jace's collar as he dragged his captive upright, remaining by the side of the car.

'Toss the film over here,' Marion instructed. 'And be careful how you throw it.'

Jace's father underarmed the canister across the space and Marion caught it in his free hand. He popped off the lid and took a long look at the film inside.

'Let my kid go,' said Mr Goodman.

Marion looked up, his face expressionless at first. His eyes slowly narrowed and his thin lips stretched into a spiteful grin.

'I don't think it's as easy as that, Bob,' he said.

Mr Goodman closed his fists tightly. The treachery wasn't unexpected, but it was still loathsome. The tension between the two men started to build up like a nuclear furnace on its way to a meltdown.

'Look at this from my perspective. Maybe this is the real film, maybe it isn't; maybe you got copies of the pictures, maybe you don't. See my problem?'

'I wouldn't do that, Marion. Not while you have Grace.'

Marion tilted his head mockingly to one side.

'You know, maybe I believe that too. But I'd feel a lot safer knowing I had your wife, your kid . . . and you.'

He snapped his fingers and both the doors on the other side of the car opened. The couple who had snatched Jace from Fair Market got out, looking every bit as unsympathetic as they had those few days before.

They advanced quickly towards where Mr Goodman stood motionless, unable to think, let along react. The hard-faced man started to reach out to grab him.

'No!' came a loud shout.

All four adults halted in their tracks. Mr Goodman had to turn to see where the shout had come from. They could all hear someone walking from the shadow of the stand into the car park.

Chris walked up behind Mr Goodman, halting just to his left. 'Julian' looked extremely unhappy to see him again. From Chris's perspective it was a pity there were no fire buckets close at hand this time.

'You've got what you came for,' he said. 'Why don't you just let Jace go?'

Marion uttered a short, brittle laugh.

'You!' he sneered. 'You're a real troublemaker, aren't you? You've been getting in my way since I first arrived in this pokey little country.' He stopped, his face severe and menacing.

'Hasn't it occurred to you that one little brat isn't going to stop me getting what I want?'

Actually, it had been uppermost in Chris's mind ever since he had shouted his challenge across the car park. When he called out, he had been hoping that a brilliant plan would jump into his head so that he could save the day. He was still waiting.

Then there was a second voice.

'How many do we need?'

Everyone turned, startled, to see who was joining in this time. The voice, with its slightly odd accent and laughing tone, had come from over by the gate. Someone was stepping out from behind the hut where the security staff normally hid during match days.

'Nicky!' cried Chris, more surprised than anyone.

'Hi!' said Fiorentini. He was walking along the next aisle, past Marion and Jace, past 'Julian' and his girlfriend. He angled between the parked cars and stood at Chris's side.

'What are you doing out here?' asked Chris.

'I don't have a ticket to get in,' replied Nicky, as if that explained everything.

Marion was looking very uncomfortable. 'What is this?' he growled. 'A boy scout camp?'

Nicky was looking very pleased with himself. He and Chris had spoken during the day and Chris had told him what was due to go down.

'I thought this meeting was supposed to be a secret . . .' muttered Mr Goodman.

'Nicky wouldn't tell anyone,' said Chris.

'Which leaves us just where we were,' hissed Marion. 'Only with one more hostage for me to drive away from here with.'

'That's not how it works,' said Nicky. 'I didn't come here on my own. My uncle brought me.'

Marion could hardly contain himself.

'Your *uncle*?'

'Fabian Fiorentini. He's a big wheel round these parts as well as being the head of the family.'

Marion was looking towards the gates to see if Nicky was bluffing. They could all just about make out the shape of another Mercedes parked across the entrance, blocking the route.

'My cousins came too,' said Nicky, careful not to specify how many. 'All of them. And we're Italian.' He looked at Chris and gave him a wide grin. 'Real Mafia . . .' he added.

Chris felt like laughing. There was no way that Marion would fall for Nicky's Mafia fairytale.

Marion, on the other hand, had never felt less like laughing. In fact, he was beginning to suffer from a real sense of humour shortage. He grasped Jace even tighter, pulling him against his chest. Mr Goodman was frozen, unable to move; 'Julian' and Mrs Julian were looking back at Marion, waiting for instructions.

Marion was trying to get back in front.

'Fine. So you've got a hundred cousins, aunties and friends of the family just outside the gate. You think that changes anything? My hired help are armed.'

He gestured impatiently at 'Julian', whose face was starting to look more blank than menacing.

'We can't shoot them all, Mr Marion . . .' he started to say.

Marion uttered a howl of rage. 'I hate this stupid country!' His face was bright red with anger and he was holding Jace so tightly Chris was worried the American might be strangled. Nicky giggled. Driving stroppy adults insane was something of a hobby of his; teachers, parents, American gangsters, they were all the same to him . . .

'It's still just one feeble man and a couple of kids! Surely you can deal with that!'

It came as no surprise when another voice joined the proceedings. Chris would have been almost disappointed if there hadn't been one iast twist.

'Excuse me, sir,' the voice said, in a studiously polite American accent. 'I think that's our team mate you're holding there. I'm going to have to ask you to let him go.'

From almost every side, people were stepping out from between the parked cars, rising up from the darkness like ghosts. Virtually every member of the Colts, all of the Mount Graham team, a few others Chris recognised . . .

Mason Williams III lined up alongside Chris and Nicky, setting his jaw squarely in that way that only American heroes can do. Nicky tried to copy him, but the grin spoiled the effect.

'Is there anyone you didn't tell about this meeting?' gasped Mr Goodman, watching as the throng closed in around Marion's car.

'I just wanted to let Jace's team mates know he was going to be safe and sound,' said Chris apologetically. He hadn't meant for them to follow, but one of them must have noticed his headlong dash down the stairs and fetched the cavalry.

Marion was looking around wildly, astonished at the sheer number of people confronting him. He must have computed the odds on escaping pretty quickly, because he suddenly lifted his hands, releasing Jace from the choking grip in which he had been held. Jace ran quickly past 'Julian' and into his father's arms. They hugged for a moment, then Jace turned round to see what Marion's next move might be.

In fact, Marion had already made it. Taking advantage of the distraction offered by letting Jace go, he had pulled the film from its container, exposing it in the light from the lamps above the car park, then screwing it up into a tiny ball and ripping it to bits.

'I take it that was the real film,' he said to Mr Goodman. 'I'm sure I would have been able to tell if you were lying.'

Mr Goodman nodded.

Marion grinned, clearly starting to feel control of the situation returning.

'So, where do we go from here? You have your son, I have what I came for. In my opinion, the bargain is concluded as agreed.'

Mr Goodman couldn't argue. What other hold did they have over Marion? There was a long silence. Marion looked around again, satisfied that there was still no sign of any police and no-one prepared to raise any objections as he moved towards the car, preparing to get back in and drive away.

'What about Mrs Goodman?' said Chris.

Marion's ill-natured smile dissolved like mist. 'What?'

'The deal was that you'd call the States and tell your associates to let her go.'

It was clear that Marion didn't like the idea of being upstaged by some British kid. He shook with rage, his eyes developing that strange diamond brilliance they had when he was severely ticked off.

'When I'm away from here . . .' he snarled.

Chris was shaking his head. 'I'm not sure we can trust you to do that, Mr Marion. Not after your stunt here this evening. I think you should make the call now.'

'What – and then you'll just let me go?'

'I'm not sure we'd be able to stop you,' Chris said. 'Since Jace's father was involved, I'm sure you'd beat any charge of kidnapping. Or you could just blame it on these two –' He pointed towards 'Julian' and his girlfriend, who were watching the cordon of people surrounding them with some anxiety. 'You can leave whenever you want.'

Marion considered this for a moment. After a lifetime covering his tracks and avoiding trouble with the law (with that one blemish on his record), he was used to having something to shield him from trouble. Chris knew that he had probably broken all kinds of laws, but maybe he had covered his tracks sufficiently.

'If that's true,' Marion said at last, 'what's to stop me leaving anyway – with or without having Mrs Goodman released?'

Chris took a pace forward. 'Because when Jace's father said he hadn't made a copy of the film, he was telling the truth. He hadn't cheated on the deal.' He pulled a brightly coloured envelope from his pocket, with its large Kodak logo, and opened it to show a thick wad of glossy prints and a small sleeve of negatives. 'I had.'

Marion was straining to see what the pictures showed, but he was too far away and the light was too poor.

'Horses,' said Chris. 'From his father's ranch. Oh, and some documents –'

'You expect me to believe they left some kid in charge of those pictures?' he cried.

'I had them done on the day Jace gave me the film,' Chris explained. 'No-one else knew.' He turned round to offer an apologetic smile to Mr Goodman. 'I'm better at keeping some secrets than others.'

He faced Marion again. The American was starting to look uncertain for the first time.

'So . . .' he whispered. 'What's *your* plan?'

'Call your people and have Mrs Goodman released. And let her talk to her husband. They can agree some kind of code, then she can call us here when she's somewhere safe. After that, you can go.'

Everyone was nodding and smiling, agreeing that this sounded like a sound plan. Marion watched the ring of people around him, clearly trying to think of a way to turn things around. No-one looked frightened of him any more and he wasn't used to that. Finally, his shoulders slumped and the sharp light went out of his eyes. There was an edge of defeat in his voice when he next spoke.

'So – what? We stand out here in the car park for a couple of hours?'

'No,' said Chris, almost scolding him for being so stupid. 'We go inside. We're still only halfway through dinner. By the way – have you eaten?'

Fifteen

The ref blew his whistle and the final game commenced.

Chris tapped the ball to Jazz, who laid it back. The Colts' midfielders strung a sequence of short, simple passes together as the Americans pressed forward. Chris moved upfield, trying to lose his marker.

On the sidelines, a small but significant band of spectators cheered the opening moves in the game as if this was the FA Cup Final.

He took a pass with his back to goal and the big American, Lowell, jammed up close, denying him space. He looked to his left and saw a Colt free on the right wing, and swivelled to hit a pass directly to the guy's feet.

'Yours, Jimmy!' he called, then signalled ahead as he spun off Lowell's challenge and ran into space. 'Jimmy' hit the return pass just a little long.

In the middle of the crowd of adults on the touchline, wrapped warmly against the chill, two adults were jumping up and down frantically. They'd never last 40 minutes like that, Chris thought. For now, though, they were cheering each throw-in as if it was the winning goal.

Chris took a long look around as he waited for the Americans to take the goal kick. The mini-tournament Sean Priest had arranged as the climax of the Americans' visit was proving quite a success. There were perhaps 100 people watching the games at the London Road training ground.

The outcome of the two games in the morning had come as a surprise to a lot of people. First the Colts had taken on a team picked from players of their age on United's youth books and won 2–0. That was a pretty good result, seeing as it was only a week since the same players had beaten the Colts 3–0.

However, it almost paled into insignificance compared to the shock that followed. Mount Graham were a goal down to Rotterdam's fluid, gifted players inside five minutes and survived by a hair's breadth when Rotterdam hit the bar three minutes later. By half-time, they were lucky to have avoided another two or three. After that sparkling performance, though, Rotterdam seemed to lose their way. A cruel deflection gifted Mount Graham an equaliser against the run of play ten minutes after the restart, after which Rotterdam played really defensively, as if they had used up all their attacking ideas.

The roar that went up when Barkley de Souza smashed in the winner from the edge of the box must have carried back to New Jersey.

Was the game fixed at half-time? Some thought so, but no-one dared ask the crestfallen lads from Rotterdam.

After lunch, the second pair of matches were played (each game was just twenty minutes each way; it meant the players could just about keep up a decent pace through all their fixtures). The Colts faced Rotterdam, with the Dutch lads clearly determined to show that the morning game was just a fluke. They hit the woodwork again – Russell Jones never saw the ball until it was on its way back off the post – and kept the Colts' defence extremely busy.

At the other end, Chris and Rory had worked hard, providing an outlet for their hard-pressed defence. The Rotterdam defenders were quick and mobile, but Chris started to find space as they pushed up and twice managed to get behind the last man as a pass was fed through, only to see both chances gobbled up by the keeper.

After half-time, Rotterdam went forward with even greater determination for the first ten minutes, but they were rattled when a quick clearance from Zak found 'Jimmy' out on the right touchline. His first-time pass had been perfectly weighted for Chris to run on to. Going round the last defender, Chris had been pushed wide, but it still took a brilliant save from the Rotterdam keeper to keep the shot out.

At the other end, Russell Jones had a blinder of a game.

When the final whistle blew, he had walked off beaming all over his face, having kept out fifteen goal-bound strikes over the 40 minutes. A draw was an insult to the skill and drive Rotterdam had shown, but the Colts were delighted. With three points from two games, they were well in the hunt to win the tournament.

Chris and his team mates had missed the fourth game, between United and the Americans (Iain Walsh wanted to have one of his 'little chats'), but everyone was talking about it afterwards. The Americans had played brilliantly, particularly a lad called Michael Kim, who scored the winner. Sadly, he was limping quite severely at the end of the match, having stretched a thigh muscle. Stefan Brodenberg had looked him over.

'A pity. I think that's your tour over.'

'I'll put a sub on for the last game,' Benford Carter had sighed. He was clearly hoping they could still win the tournament.

'I've got some stuff in the boot of my car that will help ease the pain,' Stefan told Kim as he led him off to the dressing room. 'I'll go and bring it round.'

There was a long gap after that match, to allow everyone to rest and take on some nourishment. The Americans were on a high – top of the group with four points! A draw against the Colts and they would win the challenge.

During that period before the last round of games started, Sean Priest had worn a strange expression, as if he couldn't decide whether to be delighted for his guests or annoyed with the second mediocre display from the United youth team.

'They're happy,' he had said, nodding at the Americans.

'They're better players than we thought,' Chris had replied, who was sitting nearby taking a long pull from a bottle of banana-flavoured milk. 'They've really come on this last couple of weeks.'

Priest had nodded, obviously glad that his training methods were having a good effect on somebody.

'How do you fancy your chances?' he had asked.

Chris had grinned widely. 'It'll be a great game.'

'Yes, Jazz! Now!!' called Chris as he sprinted into the gap. The two defenders hesitated, each wondering if the other would pick him up.

The pass was perfect, over one defender's head and behind Williams. Chris took it on his left foot, turned in towards goal and waited as the keeper moved off his line to meet him. At the last moment, he stroked the ball off his upper instep, firmly driving it underneath the goalie's outstretched leg and into the net.

Four minutes gone: 1–0. Mount Graham looked a little deflated, but they had come back against Rotterdam, something Mason Williams reminded his team mates about as they walked back to the positions for the restart.

Chris jogged back over the halfway line, taking the congratulations of his team mates in his stride. He paused as he went by the defender Jazz's pass had so comprehensively beaten, a tall guy whose hair was hidden under a bandana.

'Unlucky,' he told the American.

'It's not over yet,' the boy replied.

Chris ran off. His eye ran round the touchline. Quite a few of the neutrals were cheering on the Americans, but some of the Colts' families were there to watch and they were shouting and cheering wild –

The flash of red caught Chris's eye first. He did a double take and looked again. There was no mistake.

The red sports car was at the end of a line of cars about ten metres from the edge of the pitch. It hadn't been there the last time he had looked.

Marion's car. The car he had been driving when he had taken Mr Goodman to Chris's house. The car he had been conspicuously *not* driving when he turned up at Star Park to make the exchange.

Chris stared at it for a moment, until the ref's whistle for the restart made him jump. He couldn't take his eyes off the gleaming, racy shape of the car, so out of place alongside Volvos, Renaults and Fords.

It couldn't be Marion. As soon as they knew Mrs Goodman was safe, they had arranged for Marion to be taken to the airport and whisked back to the States. There had been plenty of time for him to make his way back, of course, but what would have been the point? The British police had been told everything (well, almost everything) and they would be watching out to make sure he didn't return. Also, Mr Goodman had called the American embassy in London, as well as the FBI, making sure they knew what had been going on.

Marion was out of the picture. As far as the few people who knew anything about what had been going on were concerned, that wrapped the whole story up.

Chris knew different.

The ball sailed out into touch. Chris took the opportunity to run over to 'Jimmy' Fiorentini. 'Don't look now . . .' he began (which, of course, meant that the other boy looked immediately), 'but that red sports car over on the other side of the pitch . . .'

They both knew what it meant.

'Is there anyone in it?'

'No,' Chris answered. 'At least, I don't think so. But it means trouble. Keep your eyes open. Don't go anywhere near that car.'

'Right.'

Chris moved back towards the middle, still more aware of the car than the game. A pass from Tollie went under his foot.

'Wake up, Chris!!' yelled Walsh from the touchline.

Chris shook his head and tried to get his mind back on the game. Even so, he kept looking over towards the left touchline, where the sinister shape sat hugging the ground like a predator tensed to strike.

Chris's sudden loss of concentration was causing his team mates a lot of trouble. They were used to him finding space as soon as they won possession, giving them someone they could hit a pass to as they tried to build an attack. Now, looking up, Zak found Chris heavily marked. The Colts captain was under pressure from a strong challenge from de Souza and thumped the ball vaguely in the direction of 'Jimmy', deep on the wing.

It was a wild clearance and the ball sailed over 'Jimmy's' head, the touchline and the painted boards around the pitch, landing near the groundskeeper's hut near the side gate.

'Jimmy' trotted after it. Chris took a moment to look

across once more at the bright red sports car. It was troubling him more than ever. Why would anyone continue to use something so conspicuous? Even if you thought no-one would know who it belonged to, why would you draw attention to yourself by parking it so obviously close to the touchline on that side?

Unless . . .

Chris whirled round. 'Jimmy' was a long way off, perhaps 30 metres away. The ball had landed in some spindly bushes at the edge of the training ground, beyond which there was a wire fence and then the main road.

Someone was stepping out from behind the grounds-keeper's hut.

'No!!!' yelled Chris at the top of his voice, and he took off at full speed. Everyone else was gaping in amazement. The adults on the far side of the field, by the changing rooms, couldn't even really see what Chris was so alarmed about.

But Chris knew the danger.

'Ripley!!!!' he yelled.

The man turned quickly towards Chris and so, at the same moment, did 'Jimmy'. They both appeared completely amazed. Chris was hurtling towards them like a bowling ball down an alley (and they were the pins!), his face twisted in a determined grimace. He yelled Ripley's name again, putting on an even greater turn of speed. Now that he was closer, Chris could see that there was a small hole in the fence beyond the bushes. Nothing much, but big enough, Chris assumed, that Ripley could squeeze through. He had no doubt that the car Ripley actually intended to use was safely parked outside on London Road, ready to make a getaway.

Chris was only a few strides short now. He had no doubt in his mind that this was the only chance they'd have to catch Ripley. He had to act quickly. The only thing that popped into his mind was the kind of smothering, shoulder-down hit that Jace had smacked him with a week or so ago. This wasn't *Home Alone*; you didn't take on a fit, 16-stone man with much chance of success.

Chris lowered his head and prepared to make the hit.

Jace's 'tackle' at these self-same training grounds had been a perfect example of how something that looks easy really isn't if you're not used to the sport and your opponent is. In the same way, Chris strongly believed that NFL was a matter of speed and brute strength. All he had to do was hit Ripley hard and that would be that.

He hadn't counted on Ripley moving.

The big man moved frighteningly quickly too. He stepped off one foot, turned his hips and next moment Chris's thunderous, pile-driving hit was mostly wasted on coat tails, air and hedge. Slightly surprisingly, it seemed to him that Ripley actually tried to slow him down as he went past, reaching out to grab his shoulders. Even so, Chris hit the hedge with some force, half-embedding himself in branches and leaves.

His rescue attempt was completely stuck.

All the same, Chris was a great believer in chasing after lost causes. Despite being almost upside down and jammed tight into vegetation, he yelled at 'Jimmy' to run.

'Wait . . .' started Ripley, his hand extended towards the other boy.

'Go!' cried Chris, pleadingly. It was too late, though. Ripley fastened his fingers into the other boy's shirt and held him fast.

All he had to do now, Chris knew, was drag him through the hole in the fence and make his getaway.

His mind raced through the events that would follow that awful possibility, playing them through like a feature film stuck on fast forward. Ripley would disappear until he could find some way to take 'Jimmy' to the States, giving him to Marion. Marion would start his blackmail attempt all over again, only this time . . .

'Ripley!' he yelled. 'Give it up! It won't work!'

'Give what up?' demanded Ripley, and he looked very confused. Perhaps his orders weren't clear; perhaps he was working alone.

'We've tricked you, Ripley. That isn't Jace Goodman.'

Chris had the satisfaction of seeing Ripley's face register complete shock, but there wasn't much to be gained from it. He was still tied up in shrubbery and 'Jimmy' was in his grip, struggling, but not very effectively.

'This disguise isn't –'

Chris cut Ripley off. 'We've tricked you. It isn't Jace . . . it really is Fiorentini.' He managed an upside down smile of triumph. 'Nicky Fiorentini.'

Ripley's jaw tensed. He hauled his captive round so that he could take a closer look at him. Anyone could see the difference between Jace and Nicky. In size alone . . .

Ripley glared at Nicky for a moment longer and then his face started to lose the angry stress it had worn. He started to grin. More than that, he started to laugh.

'Unbelievable,' he said, in between bursts of loud guffaws. He let go of Nicky's shirt and reached into the bushes. 'You guys are too much.' Chris tensed, wondering what was going to happen next. Ripley pulled him out of the vegetation and set him upright.

He was still laughing, making no attempt to escape as several people came closer. Chris wasn't laughing yet, but he knew that there was something here that didn't make a lot of sense.

'Twelve years I've been a cop,' said Ripley. 'And I ain't never had a case like this before.'

Oh, oh.

'You're a cop?' asked Chris. Then he realised that this question wouldn't give him a complete answer to his questions, so he added: 'A real cop?' Even that wasn't enough, but he struggled to think of a way of asking Ripley if he was also an honest cop.

'A detective with the SFPD,' Ripley replied, then spelled out what SFPD meant when he saw how confused Chris looked. Chris could hear people approaching and looked round to see Priest, Mr Carter, Stefan Brodenberg and the whole Mount Graham team among the many who had come over.

'You don't work for Marion?' asked Chris.

Ripley laughed. 'Not exactly. I've been undercover for the last few years, trying to nail him. Does that count?'

Chris found himself starting to smile nervously.

'Then . . .' Then what? He couldn't think of where to start his questions. Fortunately, with such a sizeable audience, Ripley decided to fill in all the blanks without prompting.

'We've had our eye on Marion since he came out of prison and moved to California. Our office figured he'd be up to his old tricks again, so I made contact, pretending to be on the take. I fed him some info now and again to make him think I was on his team, but mostly I kept my boss informed about what he was up to, and looked for evidence to nail him.

'Then Bob Goodman showed up and we had a problem. After the last time, he wasn't going to trust any cops, so we couldn't let him know that I was on the inside. He could have blown my cover, freaked out, anything. So, we just let the game run.

'Next thing I know, Goodman's threatening to blow the whistle on Marion and Marion's goons are after Goodman's wife and kid. So, I head out to the rendezvous point to try and rescue them.

'Trouble is, Jace has run off. So, I can't just wrap everything up neatly. I have to pretend to go along with taking Mrs Goodman hostage. Until Jace shows up, we can't do nothing else.

'Next thing I hear, Jace has made contact with his uncle and is going to fly off to England. Marion says he's going to follow him over to get the film back.' He paused, running his finger over the scar along his jaw. 'I didn't think that was what we wanted.

'So, although he doesn't want me to come along, I make my own arrangements. The thing is, I can't tell anyone who might say something. Until we have all three Goodmans and the film in the bag at the same time, Jace and his family are in danger. What Marion doesn't know is that we've got Mrs Goodman already – it wasn't his guys who were looking after her, it was mine. So, I try to keep my eye on everyone over here, but Jace keeps disappearing and Marion seems to be getting closer than me so I look for someone who can help me out.'

Chris realised who he meant. He turned to Stefan Brodenberg and offered him an apologetic smile.

'I thought you were . . .' he mumbled. Stefan laughed.

'I've never done anything criminal in my life!' he replied. 'Well, not off the field anyway.'

'Stefan was supposed to help me contact Jace, but you guys kept hiding him,' continued Ripley. 'I've got to hand it to you, that disguise thing was brilliant! I mean, Stefan saw through it right away, but when he called me, I still didn't know what we were supposed to do. At least you were one step ahead of

Marion. When he broke into your house that day, I was sure he'd find the film and that we'd be sunk.

'Before we could come up with a workable plan, Goodman grabbed Jace and – well, you know the rest. We kept an eye on the exchange, knowing that Mrs Goodman was safe and that all we had to do was make sure Marion didn't do anything cute. Well, he did, but you stopped him. Pretty neat too, I thought.'

That seemed to clear just about everything up as far as Chris was concerned. He wondered if he was going to be in any trouble for having made Ripley's life so difficult.

'What about the car?' he asked, pointing back across the pitch.

'It's a hire car. I "borrowed" it when Marion got busted by you guys. Stefan's been using it since then. Kinda like payment for services rendered.'

And he'd driven it closer to the dressing rooms when he went to get the kit he used to treat Kim's injury . . .

'One thing,' asked Priest. 'If you've got Marion locked up and all the Goodmans are safe, why are you still here?'

'That's just it,' sighed Ripley. 'We don't have the Goodmans. We thought Jace and his father would fly home, but they didn't. Stefan hasn't seen either of them for days. They vanished more or less straight after that dinner at your soccer stadium . . .'

'Ah . . .' said Chris, as a prelude to his confession. 'You see, we thought you were working for Marion and we knew you hadn't been caught . . .'

To his relief, Ripley laughed. 'You hid them again? What was it this time; another one of your cunning disguises?'

'Well, now that you come to mention it,' said Chris. One of the American players was stepping forward. 'Jace really wanted to play for Mount Graham just once. So, I'm afraid we faked that injury with Michael Kim to keep Stefan busy and –'

Jace pulled the bandana from his head. 'We thought you'd be busy watching "Jimmy".'

By now Ripley was scanning the adults for Mr Goodman. There had been no need for any cunning disguise there. Wrapped up against the spring chill and buried in the middle of the Fiorentini clan, he had been completely invisible.

Ripley breathed a long sigh of relief. 'Then that's it,' he said. 'We've got you all safe and sound. We can go back to the States.'

Chris looked around. Everyone was grinning, relieved that it was all over. Even those people who didn't have the slightest idea what had been going on looked relieved and relaxed.

Except Jace.

'Uh – do we have to go right away?' he asked.

'Is there a problem?' asked Ripley.

'Well, if it's all right with you,' said Jace, who was standing close to Mason Williams, 'I'd like to go back tomorrow with the rest of the team.'

Ripley shrugged. He had no objections. Nor, it was clear, did any of the Mount Graham team. Even Lowell was smiling, which made him look quite human.

'Besides, we've got a game to finish,' said Jace, picking up the ball. 'One-nil to you guys, I think.' He turned to his team mates. 'Come on, guys, let's kick some Limey butt.'

Everyone turned to make their way back towards the pitch. Chris caught up with Jace and dropped his arm on his shoulder.

'This is a dumb game,' said Jace, 'but I kinda like it.'

'Perhaps you could show me NFL when we come out to the States in the summer.'

Jace grinned. 'You want to get slaughtered twice?'

Chris cuffed him round the back of the head, running off ahead. 'Hey, don't get carried away, Jace. You guys are still useless at this game compared to us.'

Jace took up the challenge, laughing. 'You hear that?' he called to his team mates. 'Mr Detective thinks we don't have a chance! Let's go!'

Ripley and Sean Priest walked back towards the side of the pitch together.

'You in charge of the Brits?' Ripley asked.

'Kind of. I keep an eye on them.'

'Yeah? Well do me a favour when you come out to the States, will you? Keep an eye on that Stephens kid. He may be a whizz at this soccer stuff, but as a detective . . .'

Now you've read The Keeper, *why not catch up with Chris and Nicky in the other exciting books in the TEAM MATES series?*

OVERLAP

Top-scoring striker Chris Stephens and fiery midfield dynamo Nicky Fiorentino are the stars of their school team – best mates off the pitch and an awesome combination on it. They sweep all before them in the battle for the County Schools Cup, and the two lads celebrate one victory after another. It seems nothing can stop them lifting the cup – until the day a talent scout turns up to watch them play, and the best of friends become bitter enemies . . .

ISBN 0 7535 0080 9

THE KEEPER

Russell Jones wants to be a goalkeeper. He is a natural athlete: fast, acrobatic, with a good eye for the ball and a shrewd instinct for reading the game. Donald 'Mac' MacIntyre is a goalkeeper already, only he wants to play midfield. When these two meet, it seems they could both make their dreams come true. But there is one problem – Mac's team think Russell is a thief . . .

ISBN 0 7535 0085 X